MURDER ON MACKINAC

ROY E. AULT

Published by:
Suncoast Publishing Co.
406 N. Indiana Ave.
Englewood, FL 34223

FORWARD

When I was dating my wife, Sherrie, back in the 1950s her family attended a weeklong insurance convention at the Grand Hotel on Mackinac Island in Michigan. Upon her return she told me of the beauty of both the Island and the Grand. The first summer we were married we embarked on a camping trip which included Mackinac Island. Several years later we took another camping trip this time with our two children which included a stay on the island. When our son, Brad, turned 18 he got a job at the Grand as a bar porter. Within a few weeks the bartender quit and Brad was promoted to bartender, a job he held for two summers while attending college. Of course we were forced to take him there and pick him up and spend time on that wonderful island. A few years ago we spent a week on the island, therefore, I know it pretty well and of course did extensive research. The other locations found in the book, Englewood, Boca Grande and Gasparilla Island are the places we've lived in for over thirty years.

This is a book of fiction. I've tried hard to use fictitious names but I'm certain there is a Kirby Kitchen or a Leasil Leggit out there somewhere – my apologies.

DEDICATION

Dedicated to Sherrie, Art and Dorothy who were the first three to read the manuscript and encourage me to have it published.

CHAPTER ONE

Ira Dempsey's great-grandfather and Jack Dempsey's grandfather were first cousins. You can figure out the relationship – if you are so inclined. Something like second cousins – twice removed. There was no doubt, however, that Ira and the Manassa Mauler were kin, though the two never met. Ira tried boxing once – as a light-heavyweight during the Columbus, Ohio, Golden Gloves. He was nineteen. He fought a black kid from the Bottoms. In the first round Ira threw a left hook. The black kid countered with a straight right. Ira's left hook went one way, his nose another. Blood went all over the ring. The fight was stopped somewhere around the one minute mark. Ira never boxed again and he never had his nose fixed. It still leaned well to the right.

Ira tried college, also – Ohio State – hated it. Halfway through his first year he saw an ad from a detective agency in the Citizen - Journal. He applied and got the job. For the next twenty-five years he followed adulterers and adulteresses gathering evidence and taking pictures for divorce cases. Occasionally he'd get a missing persons or a fake injury case, which broke the monotony. For eleven years he worked for Oliver "Oily" Frankenmuth owner of Frankenmuth's Detective Agency. When Oily wanted to retire Ira bought the business and ran it for the next fourteen years. Kept the name.

He was forty-five when he went looking for a quiet place to spend a week's vacation. He brought up Mackinac Island on his computer. He booked a week at the Mohawk – saving a thousand over what it would have cost at the Grand and made the six-hour drive just in time to catch the last Arnold's Ferry to the island. The information on the computer also mentioned the island was looking for a police chief.

Ira traveled light. One small carry-on that he rolled from the ferry to the Mohawk. He'd inquired about a horse drawn taxi and when he found it was eight bucks muttered, "Horseshit, I can walk that far." Horseshit was apropos as there was a plenty of it on the street since only horses and the like were allowed on the island and no motor vehicles. He avoided the sidewalk, as it was crowded with "fudgies". Fudgies being what the locals called tourists who came for the day – maybe two, and left with five pounds of the sweet stuff.

Ira was pissed from the beginning when he found his second floor room was "no smoking" and the Mohawk had no rooms available where he could smoke. Ira was addicted to black cigars. Cheap ones. A long veranda ran the length of the second floor. It was open from end to end with two Adirondack chairs and a small table in front of each room. You could smoke there. He dropped his carry-on onto the bed and stepped outside and lit up. An old geezer and his wife were sipping gin tonics,

"Jesus, that thing stinks," the geezer coughed.

"How long you here for?" Ira asked gruffly.

"Two weeks. Why?"

"I'm here for a week, get used to it."

Ira walked downtown looking for a liquor store. He was also addicted to Crown Royal – well, not addicted like to the cigars, but he certainly liked it – mixed with Squirt, which he could hardly find anymore and found none on Mackinac. There was only one liquor store on the island and he whistled when he saw the price of a bottle of Crown Royal,

"*Jesus Christ,*" and settled on a bottle of R&R instead – and Sierra Mist for the mix.

CHAPTER TWO

When he returned to the Mohawk he found he'd forgotten to lock the door to his room – something he'd never have done in Columbus. He'd really forgotten and that bothered him. He was a PI for god's sake. Then he realized where he was and let go of it. Never again, though. The geezer and his wife were gone. He eased into one of the Adirondacks, lit a cigar and drank deeply of his R&R and Sierra Mist. It stays light forever that far north and it was three drinks later before it was dark enough to see any lightening bugs – of which there were few – but enough to intrigue him. He didn't see any in Columbus. The geezer and his wife came home from a late dinner. Mr. Geezer wheezed out to the porch and plopped his ample butt and perspiring body into the Adirondack. He pulled out an initialed handkerchief and mopped his face – two, three times, "God, it's hot up here. It's supposed to be cooler up here. It was cooler last year. It's always cooler. It's hot as home."

Ira was on his third cigar. A cigar for each drink – that was one hell of an average. He tried not to blow any smoke the geezer's way,

"Where's home?"

"Oh, a little town outside Chicago called Kankakee. I'm mayor of the son-of-a-bitch. The only time I can get away from the loonies is now. Some people bitched and griped 'cause I took off now. Christ, I haven't been out of that frickin' place in months. But, Rosetta and I come here every year for two weeks. Let the goddam town go to hell. Best two weeks in my life."

Ira heard the toilet flush, water run in the basin and then noises in the kitchenette. Shortly, Rosetta appeared. Ira had hardly glanced at her earlier. She had a gin and tonic in each hand. She was tall, slender and wore a nice dress. She must have been sixty-five. She looked refined and when she spoke you could tell it,

"Clyde, what have you been borin' this nice young man with now? I'm sure he wants to hear all about deficit spendin', potholes, parks and swimmin' pools. Clyde just loves to talk about the place – when he's away from it. I swear."

She had a slight southern accent – not Appalachian – refined.

"This is Rosetta. A man in authority once said to me, 'You know, Clyde, the best thing about you is your wife.' Pissed me off at the time, but he was right. Rosetta's family's from Alabama. The whole bunch moved north during World War Two for jobs. She was born up here, but still talks southern. But she's a keeper."

She handed a drink to Clyde and settled easily into her chair.

"I'm Ira. Thanks for the compliment. I only wish I were as young as you look."

"Why, Ira, you do know the way to a woman's …heart. Who's the lucky lady?"

"There is no lucky lady. Oh, I guess that would be any woman smart enough not to get hooked up with me."

"Why, Ira, I doubt that."

Ira had had his share of women, a couple special ones: Mickey and Ginger. Mickey hung around for four years, Ginger about the same. Never married – didn't believe it would have been right to marry with his hours. He worked anytime of the day or night, staked out for days. Didn't think it was fair for a woman to put up with it and certainly didn't want to have any kids who might never see their father for days on end. He was satisfied with the way things were.

He wasn't ugly, he knew that. Handsome? Maybe, in a rugged way. He was large. That time he boxed in the Golden Gloves, when he was nineteen, he was a light-heavyweight then. Now he was around two-forty and six-two. Lots of gray hair. Hadn't figured on having much hair at his age. His dad was bald. He had a large scar over his left eye where a perp had tried to smash his skull with the butt of a 9mm. Scar ran right down into his eyelid. Doc Morgan said a little lower and he'd been wearing an eye patch. Nose was splayed right from the fight, but not enough to make him look bad. Just added character – like the chipped front tooth. Green eyes – strange for a man. Women have green eyes. Square jaw with a good scar on it –

where he'd slipped on the ice and hit his jaw on the sidewalk – walking to the office. Nothing theatrical about that scar.

They small talked past midnight – two more drinks, two more cigars. He learned that the geezer, Clyde, and Rosetta had been high school classmates and that Clyde had once been quite the athlete. You couldn't tell it now. Ira was surprised to learn that Clyde still played tennis and two years ago was the singles champ in the state in his age group – over sixty-five. Ira didn't think Clyde could take two steps without a wheeze. Rosetta was into classical music and sang in the church choir. She had no interest in Clyde when he first attempted to woo her, but Clyde was persistent and after a two year courtship they married and that was thirty-seven years ago. They had three children, all girls. One was killed in a car collision coming home from a date. The crash occurred just a few yards from the house. Rosetta said as soon as she heard the crash she knew Jonie was dead.

Ira kept the A/C off and the porch door open all night. He had the most restful sleep in a long time. He heard Clyde coughing on the porch, early. He ignored Clyde but couldn't ignore the flock of songbirds that seemed perched on his headboard. When he opened one eye he looked for bird manure. It was 8:12 – late for him.

Breakfast was part of the deal and the Mohawk offered a good one. Ira normally was a coffee man and that was it for breakfast. But that was because he had to fix it. He had two waffles with a ton of butter and two pots of syrup, three sausage links and two cups of black coffee. When he first tried coffee while still living at home his dad had said, "Son, if you're gonna' drink the stuff, drink it black". And he had.

The day was perfect, sunny and brisk, much cooler than the day before. He hired a carriage and circled the island. It was a two cigar ride – eight and three-tenths miles. He felt good, relaxed. He hated stakeouts. He was starting to feel human. He started to whistle, something he often did as a kid, but seldom did anymore. He liked this island. He got off at the Grand,

"I'll walk the rest of the way," he told the driver and gave him a good tip. It was worth it.

He walked the long acclivity to the Grand. Even Ira was impressed with the hotel – that was not easy. Flowers on both sides marching their way slowly to the impressive six-hundred and sixty foot porch, the carriage horses clipping their way to the long case of steps leading to it. Lemon hued awnings. The dozen large American flags hanging from the veranda made him feel patriotic – that was not easy, either.

He stopped at the top and looked over the rail to the gardens below accentuating the tennis courts and the swimming pool. Rich boys and girls were showing their stuff. Women get all bent out of shape when fifty-year old men look at a fifteen-year old girl stacked like a brick shithouse. That's part of nature women will never understand. That's a man's job. It's not lechery, it's nature. When a man does not get a rise from such delectable creatures, it's time to call the wagon. It's not that they have to act on it, but they certainly can enjoy it and Ira was. He watched as a girl wearing a suit made out of less than two square feet of material did a pike off the high board. God's masterpiece was the female form. If women were smart they'd enjoy looking at that twenty-year old pool boy with equal lust. That's all he had to say on the subject.

He walked up the long staircase. He started to go in until he saw the sign, "Hotel Tours $10."

"You mean I have to pay ten bucks to see inside."

"Not, if you have lunch with us, sir, there's no charge."

"How much's lunch?"

"It's a wonderful buffet for thirty dollars, sir."

"I'll think on it," he said.

"Certainly, sir."

Ira wasn't pissed; he just wasn't ready to spend thirty dollars on lunch, anywhere on the island. He lit another cigar and walked into town. He found a place on the water and had clam chowder, a half-dozen cocoanut shrimp and a Papst Blue Ribbon. He didn't even know they made the stuff anymore. For years he drank Black Label, a Cleveland beer, but it had been gone for years. He smoked a cigar over his second Papst. I won't say how much he paid for lunch – but he could have eaten at the Grand. He blinked when he saw the bill,

"Damn, this place isn't cheap."

After lunch Ira walked the back streets to the Mohawk. On the way he saw the police station. *Might as well stop by,* he thought. He did.

It was an old wooden thing on Market Street, once part of John Jacob Astor's fur trading post. It was a national historical site but still served as the police station and had two cells. Not many places on the island were air conditioned and this wasn't one of them. All the doors and windows were open and he walked in. And there was Barney Fife.

Yes, indeed, there at the desk sat Barney Fife, incarnate. Even the damn uniform was the same, tan and with the hat and all. Only it was clear that the Mackinac Barney was much taller than the Mayberry one – but he was just as thin.

"How can I help you – don't say it."

Ira stifled his laugh but couldn't stop the big grin.

"Don't say it," the man warned, again.

"I won't, I won't. I hear the job of police chief is open here. I came in to hear about it."

"Well, it's open all right. Ralph Metcalf was the soul of this department for over thirty years. Drowned trying to unfoul his prop from a lobster-pot line. No one really knows what happened. Had a big cut on his forehead. Interested?"

When he spoke all traces of Barney Fife were gone. His voice resounded with authority. He was articulate and intelligent – you could tell from his speech.

"I don't know. How about you? Have you applied for the job?"

"Not me. I'm happy doing what I'm doing. And I don't have to take all the grief that the chief does. Not there's that much. But more than you think. Every time a horse poops on the street and someone's not out there with a shovel they call us – sometimes on 911. Besides, I've got a great wife and two teenagers that I want to spend time with before they go off and leave the island. I'm Officer Dickerson – Ed. People who know me call me, Slim," and he stood and offered his hand.

Ira took it and it was a very firm handshake,

"Ira Dempsey. Don't say it. Are you *it*, now?"

"Nope. There's Doug Upland. He came here a dozen years ago as a bar porter at the Grand. Lasted about a week. Those boys and girls *work* at the Grand. Doug wasn't into work. Came back the following year and the same thing happened. You'd think they'd learn at the Grand. He was twenty-one. Stopped at the police station and asked for a job. Ralph took one look at him and decided he could use a man of his stature. Two weeks later he was sorry he hired him – but he never let him go. We don't have much in common, but we tolerate each other."

"Where's he?"

"Since Chief Metcalf died we take turns, one week he's on nights and the next week it's me. This is his week. We each do six to six. When Chief was alive we split things up three ways and alternated more. Be glad to get a third in here, but the board moves like democracy – if you know what I mean."

"Where can I get an app?"

"See Janet over there," he said. motioning with his head toward an office where a plump and pleasant lady sat. She had graying hair and made no attempt to color it. "Take me as I am." Even though the door was open he knocked,

"Here. I heard you talking to Ed. Fill out both sides. Where you stayin'?"

"At the Mohawk."

"Put that down, and the room number. The board interviews whenever they feel like it so put down when you're leavin'. When is it that you're leavin'? "

"Not this Sunday, but next."

"That's good, that'll give the board plenty of time to have you come in."

Ira filled it out as directed and handed it to her,

"Nice meeting you, Janet, I hope to see you again."

"Oh, I'm sure you will. The board is interviewing anybody – well, you know what I mean."

Ira nodded his head in the affirmative and then walked over and shook Officer Dickerson's hand,

"Nice meeting you, too, Officer Dickerson and good luck. I hope you get a chief soon."

"Same here. Me, too."

CHAPTER THREE

For the next several days Ira played the tourist. He continued to chow down for breakfast at the Mohawk. He frequented the fudge shops and found the fudge was damned good and he had some from every shop. Murdick's, especially. Just down from the Grand, on a back street, was a bakery that sold the largest cinnamon rolls a man ever saw. And the best a man ever tasted. He got into the habit of stopping there after he'd walked off his breakfast and before lunch and having one, along with excellent black coffee – not boomer coffee, mind you, just great regular black coffee. He didn't eat much lunch – whatever junk food that appealed to him – corndogs, hamburgers, hotdogs, a slice of pizza. That's what he ate when on a job, anyway. Why mess up a good thing. Cholesterol didn't concern him. After seeing the prices on the island, thirty dollars didn't seem too bad so he had lunch one afternoon at the Grand. The food was excellent and the service superb. It was worth the thirty bucks. He heard about the head chef, Henri Petri – French – who'd been there seven years and evidently was very demanding of the kitchen. No one liked him. In the evenings Ira smoked a bunch of cigars, drank a lot of R&R and switched to Sprite for his mix.

He took every tour, walked every path, learned to drive a horse and carriage, went horseback riding once and that was enough – the inside of his thighs were raw and the surrounding muscles ached for two days. He rented a bicycle – once, also. He was smart enough not to try the eight and three-tenths miles trip around the island, but did ride most of the day in town and found the uphills were in far greater proportion than the downhills. That was the end of that. The weather was Chamber of Commerce stuff. He, Clyde and Rosetta continued talking on the veranda after dinners. He learned a lot – we'll go into that later. Well, one thing he learned was their last name was Stone and he said, "Rosetta Stone?" and she said, "Yes, and that's the reason I didn't want to get hooked up with him. My maiden name was Burbank. Most people call me 'Podie' anyway so the name didn't bother me much. I don't know where the Podie came from."

The afternoon he had come back to his room from the bicycle farce he flopped on his bed. His legs felt like a couple of matchsticks. On the way down he saw the flashing red light on the telephone. He was asleep instantly and it was well past dusk before he heard Clyde and Rosetta clink their gin and tonics together. He'd missed dinner. He picked up the phone, "You have a message – push 1 on your telephone key pad." He did.

"Say, honey, this is Kathyrn McCormack. Most call me Katy. I'm mayor of the 'Gem of Lake Huron'. That's what I call this place. I think I saw you riding your bike today. I don't miss much. You didn't look real happy. Try shanks ponies, it's easier. You're at the Mohawk, where that old coot, Clyde Stone, stays. Comes up here every damn year and tries to tell me how to run this place, as if Kankakee was anything like my town. But he's harmless and I listen. I don't shut him up. Say, honey, Ed tells me you've applied for the job of chief of this august force. We're meetin' tomorrow night at seven in the town hall. If you can make it we'd be pleased to ask you some questions. Hear you're a gumshoe. Well, I have nothing against gumshoes. Se ya'."

Something had told Ira to pack a white shirt, tie, blue blazer and gray slacks. That's what he wore to the interview. He'd forgotten to pack dress socks. All he had were white and they did not look cool but Ira managed to keep his pants legs close to his shoe tops all night. Kind of like a girl keeping her legs crossed in company. Kathyrn "Katy" McCormack was outlandish. Ira was certain he'd seen her on the streets since he'd arrived. She was tall and reed thin with wild red hair – all Irish. Freckles and burnt skin, sixtyish, been mayor for thirty-four years. Wore a flowered dress to the tip of her shoes, which were flats and had thin white socks. I was going to say her hat was indescribable – but one must, so, it was straw, large, had cloth of colors all over it and if it had a price tag hanging down would have looked like Minnie Pearl's. Katy and the five town commissioners made up the search committee.

They asked him about his agency – why was he willing to leave it. How long did he think he'd stay if offered the job? Could he live on forty-thousand a year as that's what the job paid and there did not seem to be much in the way of raises. He would have full health insurance benefits (one would think so), a car to drive – one of seven vehicles on the island – even Katy did not have a car, a uniform allowance, fourteen days off but worked all the holidays, promise of a pension if he lived long enough, a gun, bullets, badge, and two officers to manage.

"We want to wrap this up by the end of July so the new man can have a few weeks under his belt before the Labor Day shenanigans," stated Commissioner Ross Gray.

"Sounds good to me," stated Ira.

His nine days were up Sunday. Saturday night he invited the Stones to dinner. They ate at the Island House. Good food and the hostess, a girl of perhaps seventeen, was as fair a creature Ira had laid eyes on. Rosetta noticed,

"Beautiful, huh? Maybe a slight bit young for you? You are familiar with San Quentin Quail?"

Ira demurred.

They sat in the Adirondacks until well into the morning. Ira smoked and swizzled and no one objected to his cigar. He slept in and almost missed breakfast. He did miss the checkout at eleven but there was no charge. Someone said he might be the next police chief. He said goodbye to Rosetta and Clyde.

"Those damned cigars still stink," Clyde said without malice.

"They do, but I love the man," Rosetta said and gave him a hug. Ira thought it would have been nice if she were twenty years younger or he twenty years older. He wasn't sure.

"I'll be here the same time next year," Ira said. He felt genuine affection for the couple.

"We always come these same two weeks. Beats the heat of Kankakee – and the idiots. I don't know. I've got an election in November, maybe the idiots will vote me out," Clyde said with almost a wish in his voice.

CHAPTER FOUR

Ira pulled his carry-on down to the boat terminal and put it in a locker. He hired a carriage for one last ride around the island. He was not in a hurry. He liked the place. Yes, he could be the chief there – if they offered. He farted the rest of the day away and caught the last ferry to Mackinaw City. His Jeep Cherokee wouldn't start and he had to have it jumped. When it started, he saw he'd left the dome light on. It was past noon before he pulled out of the parking lot. He was at his office by seven that evening.

He had a pile of mail, a phone full of messages and though he was not much with computers he had eighty-seven e-mails, seven concerning male enhancement and four offering him oxycotin and Valium. He was yet to need the enhancement, but there were days when a Valium would have been welcome – oxycotin for certain.

Mrs. Barnhart, wife of the mayor of Columbus, suspected her husband, Jack, of banging his personal secretary, Rita. Would he put a tail on him? Well, yes, but the tail would be him as Ira was a one man operation….. The president of Ohio State University called. The football coach, Bruce Earle, was spending a lot of time at Beulah Park and Scioto Downs. Was he being influenced by the low-life that hung around the track? Was he losing large sums of money? Was he in hock to them? Would he throw a game to pay off has debts? What was going on?..... The Reverend LeRoy Helms was suspected of ripping off millions from his flock – any way to find out?..... Janet Storts had called and wanted to find her lost Jack Russell terrier. She had three kids ages nine, seven and four who were heartsick. She suspected her husband of leaving the gate open purposely. Was there any way of finding out? Those were the best ones.

After going through his messages he didn't know where to start so he propped his feet on the desk and lit the blackest cigar you've yet to see. He kept a bottle of Crown Royal in his right lower desk drawer, behind the files. It was an old metal desk that Oily had bought at the army surplus store. He poured some, not much, in his coffee. He liked it. Old timers called it Irish coffee. Young people don't know of it. The phone rang,

"Dempsey."

"Mr. Dempsey this is Mayor McCormack – Katy. We took a vote right after you left and voted you to be the next police chief of Mackinac Island. Interested?"

"Yep."

"Good, when can you start?"

"When do you need me?"

"Yesterday, but we'll settle on the end of the week."

"Well, I've got a business to get rid of."

"Something tells me you're just the guy who can do it. People are probably falling all over themselves to buy such a business. Need you by Friday. Else we go to plan B."

"Mayor, you don't know me well, yet." And he hung up the phone.

Ten, nine, eight, seven, six, five, four. Ring. He answered.

"Take all the time you need."

"I'll be there Friday, but I wanted you to know I'm my own man."

"Understood. I like that kind of man."

Ira put the business up for sale. He had a nephew who knew computers and they put it on Craig's list, Mary's list, John's list and the Queen of Sheba's list. Also in the Citizen-Journal, where he'd seen Oily's advertisement twenty-five years earlier,

Must sell by Friday, Great PI business, oldest in city, license transferable, set your own hours, (that was a damn lie), good pay, exciting work (debatable). Financing available. Phone 473 – 2110. Ask for Ira.

One call. Some dork from Reynoldsburg. Ira could tell he was a dork. Had a speech impediment, too. Sounded like a cleft palate. Ira didn't care who he sold to, but the guy never called back, never came to the office. By Thursday it was obvious no one wanted to be the next Mike Hammer, so he called his landlord, Harold Rose, and asked him how much to pay off the lease. In spite of some lean times, Ira had never missed the rent,

"Forget it Ira. Give me a month's rent so I can look for someone. I've got a stepson who teaches school and plays guitar. He's been want'n to teach guitar. So he might be interested. Where'n hell you goin'?"

"That's white of you, Rosie. Tell you what. I'll leave all my stuff here but my files and you can give it all to an auction house and make a little off it. Mackinac Island. They want me to be the chief of police and I can't think of a better place to work until retirement. Nothin' ever happens there."

In spite of all the phone messages Ira never had more than a handful of clients at once. He was working on a half-dozen cases. He called them and referred them to Israel Wolfe, scion of the Wolfe family who owned the Columbus Dispatch and made governors and senators. Israel was the black sheep of the family. He didn't go into the newspaper business, but he was a good PI and Ira had no problem giving up his clients to him. He called Mrs. Barnhart and told her he guessed husband Jack was probably banging his secretary and a few others and to call Israel. He left a message for the OSU president and said: lots of good people like to see horses run. The man's under intense pressure. Cut him a little slack.

Daisy Chain, Ira's landlady where he rented a furnished double on Blake Ave in the Short North, was not quite so understanding,

"Dammit, Ira, it's the middle of summer. I won't be able to rent that place 'til fall. And then I'll get eight students who will want to rent it. Four boys and four girls and all they'll do is screw and snort coke."

He gave her three months rent, "That should last you until school starts."

It didn't take Ira long to pack. He didn't own much. He loved coins and had a great collection. When he was staking out he'd take a few coins along and look at them with his magnifying glass while he waited for the lady to show up or whatever happened next. When he was really whipped and nothing about any case was going straight he'd get his collection out, light up a cigar, pour a hefty chuck of

Crown Royal and look at his coins. All his frustrations were gone in an hour. Most of his collection was in a safety deposit box at the Huntington, especially his 1893S Morgan Silver Dollar. There were only seventy-seven thousand of them minted. He'd paid three grand for it and that was a bargain as it was an EF-40. He packed some coins to take, but left most in the bank.

His clothes collection was far less than his coins in number and style. You've seen the snowbirds as they drive south with the rod hanging across the back seat and their clothes swinging on it. Well, that's what Ira did. Anyway, he'd be in uniform most of the time. Though he was attached to dogs, pets were out as he was gone half the time and if he left one in the apartment while he was gone there'd be crap all over the place. No dogs, no furniture. A Bose radio, the best computer money could buy, but he still took pictures the old fashioned way – with a Pentax and plenty of flashes. He loved to catch a couple in bed and scare the crap out of them when the flash went off. He bought two boxes of black Roi Tans, a case of Crown Royal and three twelve-packs of Squirt, as he knew he'd never find it on the Island, nor in Mackinaw City. Probably Detroit to find it and he'd never drive down there. Talk about crime.

Ira left Columbus late afternoon Friday. He drove straight through and drove NASCAR the last fifty miles in order to catch the last ferry. He had no idea what he was going to do with the Cherokee – he'd worry about that later. Though he'd packed light he had much more than a carry-on so he stuffed what he didn't need into a pay locker at the ferry terminal and walked to the police station. It was a few minutes before midnight. The station was deserted. He wrote a note, "I was here Friday, where were you?" signed his name, laid it on the doorstep and put a concrete block on top. Then he walked to the Mohawk.

The Mohawk is family run and the mister was on duty, half asleep and looking at a girlie magazine –at the Mohawk, no less,

"Thought I might see you again, Chief. Don't have a thing available. Don't think there's a thing in town, but you can sleep on the couch, it pulls out. We got extra blankets. And a pillow. No charge and you know 'bout breakfast."

"Thanks, that'll do. I wish breakfast was now. I'm starvin'."

"Well, look in the little fridge here. There's stuff in there and a couple beers, too. I'll make up the couch and then I'm goin' to bed. No sense in stayin' up."

"Thanks."

"Well, this should be worth a speeding ticket," and he laughed.

CHAPTER FIVE

He slept in his clothes and had no idea where he was when he awoke. He didn't hear cars tearing up and down High Street. He didn't hear anything. He looked at his watch – 3:07 a.m., but it was light and he smelled coffee. He looked again – 3:07.

Damned battery's quit and I bet there's not a place on this fricking island I can get a battery. He got up. Where could he clean up?

Jack Walsh, that was the mister. He was more than the mister, he was the owner along with Flo, his wife. They had an impressive staff, but Jack ran the front desk most of the time, especially in the evening. Wanted to be around the money. Helped at breakfast, too. So did Flo. They bought the Mohawk twenty some years ago. It was not large, just big enough to make them a decent living – the rooms weren't cheap.

"The guy in 207's gone fishin'. Early. So you can go in and clean up there," Jack handed him a key.

"He won't mind?"

"Hey, you're the police chief. What are you going to steal? I don't have anything until Monday, but you can have the couch. Monday I have a room. You can look around at the other places."

Ira showered and shaved with the fisherman's razor. His clothes didn't smell so good, but he wanted to get to the station – but not before breakfast. He had a double stack of griddle cakes, a double order of Canadian bacon and swilled two cups of coffee after lighting one of the Roi Tans. He walked to the station.

This time when he walked in instead of Ed Dickerson he was met by a giant of a man – six-five at least – two-ninety, but he looked soft. He wasn't hard and a smaller man could move him. The giant was draped lazily in the chair and over the desk and it was hard to tell where the man ended and the chair and desk began,

"You must be Officer Upland."

"Yep, and you are?"

"Ira Dempsey, Chief Dempsey."

"Oh, yeah, I got your note. I went down to Howard's to get a pack of cigarettes. You should've stayed around. I'da been back in a minute."

"I was tired."

"The chief's office's over there," the big man said, motioning with his head to a room with large glass windows that looked out on the rest of the offices. It had a glass door as well. Couldn't hide anything from anyone. "Ralph Metcalf, Chief of Police, Mackinac Island" was still on the door. You'd think with all that glass there'd be an outside window, but there was not. There was a gray metal desk, phone with an intercom, a worn chair, several file cabinets, a state of the art computer, fax machine, hall tree, digital wall clock, head of a buck deer with a nice rack, and pictures of Ralph's family. Evidently no one had come to claim them. He sat down. Tried the intercom and got Janet's office, only she wasn't in yet. Digital clock read 8:48.

"What time's Janet come in?" he kind of yelled. No one answered. He walked to the door and looked out. Officer Upland was gone. At eight fifty-five Janet Phinney walked in. That answered that question.

"Well, it's good to have a full force again – good to have a chief. We've got along okay, but it's good to have someone in charge. Welcome. Anything, I mean anything, I can do to help you, let me know."

"Thanks. Okay. How about writing down your hours on a piece of paper and sticking them on my desk. The hours of officers Upland and Dickenson, too, if you would."

"Sure."

Just about the time Janet got the "Sure" out, in walked Katy McCormack. Another wild, flowered dress – blues, reds, yellows and down to the floor. Big hat with artificial flowers. A sight.

"Chief Dempsey."

"Mayor McCormack."

20

"Saw Upland heading for doughnuts, said you got in late last night but didn't stick around. Made it by Friday, though. Here's Ralph's old uniforms. He was kind of your size. If you can fit into them wear them until we can get you some new ones. Have to go down to Cheboygan to get them."

"Speaking of sticking around, what's his hours? I'm not certain I want to put on a dead man's uniform."

"Superstitious? And I don't know his hours."

"Not really, just rather have my own. Are they clean?"

"Just now got them out of the cleaners," and that was probably true as they were wrapped in cellophane,

"I'll think about it."

"Well, no one will know who you are if you're not in uniform."

"I'll think about it."

"Here's the keys to the patrol car. One car, so you'll have to share. Cars aren't big on the island. Bikes are good around here and we've got one for each of you – good bikes. So's the car. It's not new but it's a powerful son-of-a-bitch. No one to outrun around here, anyway. Well, I gotta' go. The gun's in the safe. So's the badge. Janet's got the combination. She'll show you around. I'm sure Upland'll be back as soon as he kills a couple of doughnuts. Got a meeting. Oh, we use horses when it snows."

He got the combination and the gun – a Glock 9mm, got the tour, tried the uniform on in the john – a tight fit, but he did want the people to know he was the chief and decided he could put up with it a couple weeks. The patrol car was out behind. A big Ford LTD with a souped-up engine. They weren't expected to use it except when really needed. Bikes were the thing. He thought he might look a little foolish on a bike, but this was a retirement job – go with the flow. He cranked up the Ford and took her around the island. Got a few stares, some inquisitive, some resentful and some of annoyance – vacationers don't want to see cars, especially vacationers on horses, but the horses are old and come from Amish country and they aren't going to bolt.

Officer Upland was sprawled on the chair and desk when he returned – reading the Mackinac Island Town Crier – a weekly, full more of ads than news. A note on his desk read,

I work from 9 – 5 and eat my lunch at my desk. I'm on duty for eight hours. Answer every call including the 911's of which we get several for people will call us if they see horse poop on the street. A real emergency! Officers Upland and Dickerson have been on 12 hour shifts since Chief died. They change every week. They go from 6 to 6. Last night was the switch so Officer Upland will have been on duty 24 hours straight at 6 tonight.

Ira looked out on the rest of the offices. Janet was banging away on an old typewriter – *wonder why she didn't use the computer?* Officer Upland looked like he was having sex with the desk, he'd enveloped it. How to tell him to shape up without pissing him off. He'd been on duty sixteen hours – for what it was worth. Ira stood and stuck his head out the door,

"Officer Upland – Doug – you're gonna' get that desk pregnant if you don't get off it. You know, sit up straight – like your Mamma told you."

The big man was startled, damned near dropped his paper, reddened and then slowly unwound from the desk and chair and kind of sat up. Ira ambled out, drew up an extra chair and sat beside him,

"Hey, I know you're tired and bored, but we have to look semi-professional. It's been a long haul. You married?"

"Yeah."

"Well go on home and scare the missus. Don't come back until Janet calls you. I need the experience and you need the rest. We'll try and get on eight-hour shifts. What's a good schedule?"

"Well, when Chief was here we'd rotate by the week, one from six to two, another at two to ten and then ten to six."

"That sounds good. I'll stay to midnight and have Officer Dickenson come in 'til eight and you can have the eight to four shift. For a week. Any little Uplands?"

"What? Oh, yeah! Four. Boys. Drive Kimberly crazy. Thanks. I ain't had any regular daytime hours since Chief died."

"Go on, get out of here but when you come back sit up straight."

"Yeah."

The big man folded his newspaper and ambled out. Ira walked to Janet's office and sat down at the extra chair.

"Why do you use a typewriter? Can't you use the computer?"

"Well, a lot of our forms can't be filled out on the computer, at least the way it's programmed now. I have to type 'em."

"We'll change that in a hurry. Typing is a waste of time, energy and money."

"Well, that would be nice."

"Fill me in on Labor Day weekend. They said they wanted a chief in place before Labor Day weekend. What's the big deal?"

"Well, it *is* a big deal here. It's the end of the season. Everything closes down after the holiday. People come over here by the thousands for the weekend. Everyone works like hell for three days. Monday night there are fireworks to rival anything you've ever seen and most of the tourists are drunk. It takes a day or two to sober them up and clear them out. Then everyone works like hell for two or three more days to get things closed down and on the last day of work which will be like a Tuesday. Wednesday all the staffs of all the hotels and restaurants throw a big party up on the hill and most get drunk and do dumb things and there is a lot of sex – all over the island."

Ira found housing expensive. No way could he afford to purchase a home or even rent one. Janet informed him of Darlene Wilder, a widow, who probably had a room to rent – with kitchen privileges. It was on Mahoney Avenue, within easy walking distance of the station. Darlene's husband, George, had been a captain for the Arnold Transit Line. Several years earlier he was coming from the mainland and was about ready to dock when he had a heart attack. One hand froze on the wheel, the other on the throttle. Before the first-mate could pry his hand off the throttle George managed to plow into the Arnold dock doing over two million dollars in damages to Arnold facilities and ship. Seventeen people were injured, three seriously and were hospitalized. George was only forty-seven and was making enough money that Darlene did not need to work. And just like that her source of income was shut off and shortly thereafter she started taking in boarders.

Darlene was fiftyish, with cropped black, black hair, (dyed), a great figure and a chain smoker. She was not thin but her face was. She had a sharp nose and chin but merry eyes. She had a good sense of humor and liked people. She screened her boarders and most of the time it was one happy family unless someone screwed up her two-thousand dollars worth of washer and dryer in the basement. She liked burnt toast with peanut butter and hot chocolate for breakfast. The entire house smelled of smoke. This was great as far as Ira was concerned as he would have no qualms about smoking his Roi Tans.

It was a large house, wooden, white, with plenty of gingerbread – built in the twenties.

She was glad to have him, as most of her boarders were leaving at the end of the season. She had a small bedroom available but promised him the largest in the house when everyone was gone. He had a high bed, nightstand, antique dresser, armoire and wash stand with a pitcher and bowl. There was a bath at the end of the hall with a tub. He bought a small refrigerator for his Squirt and beer. The kitchen was as modern as the rest of the house was old. Darlene had it remodeled and installed top of the line stainless-steel appliances, including the best microwave money could buy. It received heavy use from the boarders. There was a huge basement where boarders could put extras and contained the new washer and dryer – commercial sized. They were used even more than the microwave and Darlene charged fifteen-dollars a month for the use of each – whether or not you used them. Her rent was not inexpensive, but acceptable. Ira removed his belongings from the lockers at Arnolds and settled in. His room opened upon a small porch as did the larger room he would soon have. He smoked his cigars there.

The first day he had any spare time he went to Mackinaw City. He had one huge bill for parking but found an old garage about ready to fall down where he could park the Jeep. The rent was right.

CHAPTER SIX

August was fairly quiet. He found that Slim Dickerson was as professional as any officer of the law he had ever encountered and possessed a brilliant mind. He was wasted on the Mackinac Island force. Ira was able to get Doug Upland to sit somewhat straighter and from having intercourse with his desk. He drove to Cheboygan and was measured for a new uniform. He ordered two. They came just before Labor Day. He eschewed the bike most of the time. Have you ever seen a two-hundred forty pounder on one of those little bicycles? The seat was so small it about went up his butt. The first thing he did was purchase a large seat with a sheepskin cover. He eschewed the bike, that is, until Katy McCormack came in and said, "We don't have enough in our budget for you to drive that damn big Ford all over the island. Use the bike."

He was there for retirement – no big deal, but he refused to wear the helmet. "Makes me look like an asshole."

He busted four kids from the Mohican who were racing down Cadotte Hill on their bikes. They damned near ran over a Q-tip and her husband. They came so close and so fast she threw her sack of fudge straight up,

"Goddam vandals," she hollered. Ira was coming the other way when they whizzed by. They saw him out of the corner of their eyes and started to outrun him until he laid into his whistle and hollered, "If you run I'll put your asses in the cell. If you stop it's only a small fine." They stopped.

There was an inebriation every night no matter who was on duty, either a seasonal worker or a tourist. Ira told Upland and Slim to walk the seasonals to their dorm, take them to their room if need be but not to hassle them unless they were belligerent – their penalty would come at six in the morning when they had to drag out of bed. If they were nasty and male, a friendly poke in the groin with a baton usually was enough to do the trick. For the girls it was, "What would your father think?" and that was ordinarily enough. These were good kids and came from good families.

The tourists were treated well, also. Most were vacationers – men who had one beer too many. For the ladies it was an extra margarita on the rocks with lots of salt. Neither was dangerous, mostly noisy and their kids and spouses would be pissed off and that was punishment enough for most. Again the officers escorted them to their hotel and turned them over to the night clerk. The Grand could see them coming and usually sent a valet down to help the happy party. That was just about the time the happy party barfed, sometimes on the valet and sometimes on himself and hopefully on the asphalt.

He was called once to the Grand where an enraged Chef Henri Petri had a large butcher knife pressed against the jugular vein of some poor, quaking kitchen flunky. Henri was screaming in French with a tad of English and you could make out that "thees embeecile has ruined my broths, ruined it completely and I need eet now. Now! And eet is ruined. You stupid little conch. I should kill you." and Ira was afraid he would. Henri was wild eyed and shaking like a wet dog. Ira tried to calm him down with no effect. Soft words weren't working. When Ira walked his way Henri turned toward him with the butcher knife poised over his head. Ira did not think long. With his left hand he grabbed Henri's wrist holding the knife and at the same time hit Henri flush on the jaw with a straight right. Henri went down like a sack of French fries. The Manassa Mauler would have been proud,

"Carry him to his room. Tell him I'll not file charges, but next time not to get so dammed worked up over 'broths'."

Ira was introduced to Mayor McCormack's thirty-two year old nephew, Freddie. Freddie was touched in the head – somewhat. Ira wasn't certain from what or why. He was not a psychologist or even a psychiatrist so he did not guess. It was obvious Freddie was touched.

"He's my sister Rose's boy. Illegitimate. She never married anyone and never said who the father was. Rose was killed four years ago in a motorcycle accident. She always said things were so damn slow on this island so she kept a big Harley Hog in the city. She was just a bit of a thing, but she'd get on that damned bike and open it up. Hit a rural mail carrier's car head on. She was passing a truck at about ninety. The mail carrier was stopped, putting letters in the box and when he looked up here came Rose going like a bat out of hell. It was clear and dry. No one knows what went wrong. She just ran into him – flew over the handlebars and landed forty feet down the road. Had a helmet on but it split like a watermelon and her head, too, and I don't care to talk about it. She was the only family I had and I inherited Freddie, here, and do my best with him. He loves town. Goes over every day on the first boat and comes back on the last. Just walks the town. Knows everyone. Takes peanut butter sandwiches with him."

Freddie was not obese. He was bulbous. Maybe bloated would be a better description. He looked as if he'd deflate if someone stuck a pin in him. His face was as round as a balloon. Kind of like the Michelin Man. He kept his head shaved which did nothing for his appearance. He tried to grow a beard and mustache but could do neither. Little wisps of hair clung to his chin and upper lip. He lisped. "Tho hith wordths kind of thounded like thith." Ira never saw him without a backpack. Everyone said he was harmless.

Labor Day weekend was all it was cracked up to be. Fudgies came by the thousands. The streets were jammed with people walking, people on bicycles, on horses and in carriages. Ira was certain that from Saturday through Monday midnight the island set a record for horseshit – "road apples" as the kids liked to call them. Kid stuff. Monday night there was a pyrotechnical display that was three times as good as Columbus' Red, White and Boom for July 4th. Drunks? Well, it looked after dark like the fudgies turned into alkies. Ira had both officers on duty all weekend and the three of them were overwhelmed. They tried at least to walk the drunks to their hotels – that is those who cooperated – and most did. Some didn't, some were belligerent, some threw punches – none connected, even Upland was able to stay out of the way of a haymaker. Those offenders were hustled down to the jail and both cells were crowded every night, even after turning everyone loose in the morning. They had to practically hose out the cells for a lot of the drunks lost their fudge. By Tuesday night the island was practically deserted. Everyone who was left spent the rest of the week sobering up and closing up.

Saturday night after Labor Day was the official end of the season. By Friday night the kids were starting to celebrate. For twelve weeks they had toed the line, more or less. They'd done their job. Were up at six and stumbled into bed at midnight, thoroughly exhausted. As the weeks went by more and more kids quit and it was nearly impossible to hire new people so the old ones sucked it up and just worked more. They'd spent countless hours catering to the tourists from far and wide – serving them, cleaning up after them, catering to their slightest whims and all for minimum wage and the hopes of some really good gratuities at the end of the season. Most did it cheerfully. But they'd had enough, they were ready to let go and by glory they did. Ira didn't know where so many under aged kids were getting liquor but they were and they were drinking it.

They collected a big pile of wood up on "Watch Your Step Hill" and had one hell of a bonfire. Sparks flew thirty feet in the air. Boys were in cut-offs, flip-flops and no shirts. Girls were in shorter cut-offs, flip flops and no shirts. That is to say the boys would yell out, "Show us your tits." They got this from watching TV coverage of the Mardi Gras. Well it didn't take much urging and up would come the shirt or down would go the halter – so they might as well not had a top on. Teens drink little other than beer, but they had cases of it.

The favorite thing to do other than to have sex was to ride down Cadotte Hill as fast as they could. There were all kinds of bikes: skinny tired, racers, bikes with fifteen speeds, balloon tired – it made little difference for no matter what kind of bike you were on once you started down Cadotte Hill those sons-of-bitches would fly. Of course half the riders were drunk and so there were a multitude of crashes and spills. The EMT's on the island just stayed at the bottom of the hill and picked them us as they crashed. It would have been impossible to arrest all those who raced from top to bottom so Ira arrested none, instead telling them if they came down again, "I'll nail your little butt."

Another fun thing was to race bikes around the island. This took longer but it was somewhat safer. Only four kids sailed off the road into the lake and their buddies pulled them out. The kids had cases of beer stashed along the way –so they'd ride from one cache to the next and by the time they completed the trail around the island most were roaring drunk. There was a lot of fornicating on that trip. Fornicating, of course, was the most popular of pleasures and a lot of it was going on. It would have been interesting to know how many babies were born in early June from these conjoinings. Hopefully, most used contraceptives. Ira saw right away that most of what was going on was beyond his control. Something to work on for next year!

There were only a few altercations – most of the kids knew each other – they were friends, except for the occasional boys who rubbed each other wrong – a couple of girls, too. But by the time they got to fighting they were too drunk to hurt each other and not much came of it.

Partying was still going strong at four a.m. Things slowed down a great deal by five and with the coming of dawn everything stopped. Kids slept until late afternoon, woke with thumping heads and dry mouths. Ice water was in great demand. Most had to be off the island that day – they were no longer employed. Everywhere, the young were gathering up their meager belongings and heading for the docks. There was a traffic jam at all three ferry lines by late afternoon as many parents had come to pick up their kids, just in time to drop them off at college. By nine o'clock the village was a ghost town.

Ira blew a sigh of relief. He didn't like what had occurred. Didn't like it at all and was determined not to let it happen next year. What bothered him the most was that many of the kids he'd been close to – those who were wild eyed and rabid did not have the smell of alcohol on them. They'd been into drugs – big time. He wondered where the supply had come from. *It's an island for god's sake. Had to be boats for damn sure.*

CHAPTER SEVEN

Leaves turn early on Mackinac. By the time the fudgies and workers had cleared out there was a hint of fall. Greens turned to ambers, golds, scarlets, chartreuse and dusty browns. The leaves hung like pendants waiting to be plucked by a winter god. The first good rain would send them skittering to the earth. They would cover the hillsides and valleys. The first hard frost came on the first day of fall. The island was quiet. Ira relaxed. On a bright day he took a bike ride, official, around the island. Looked for spots drugs could be brought in – there were too many. Observed no crimes.

Katy McCormack promoted a bike race around the island for the locals. One-hundred forty entered. There were no classification – any old bike would do. John McClelland was the winner. Well, he and his son, George, won – they rode a tandem. Katy ruled them out for next year.

On the twenty-third of September Ira took breakfast at the Railroad Car. It looked its name. It was out of place for there had never been a railroad on Mackinac. Nevertheless there it was – on rails, too. He was finishing a plate of two eggs – hard, hash and wheat toast. Fran, the waitress, poured him his third cup of coffee. He was the only one at the counter when a man came in and sat beside him.

"You don't know me from Adam, but you will. I come out of the woodwork this time every two years. Name's Kirby Kitchen. I'm the town mortician. Youda've run into me sooner or later – in your line of work, although the past chief only shot one person in sixteen years and he didn't die. Anyway, like I said I come out of the woodwork every two years and run for mayor. Have done so seventeen times. Lost every time. Was close in ninety-six. Lost by sixteen votes. Pretty good considering there's only five hundred on this island, about three hundred registered voters and only about half vote. Katy McCormack is a piece of fluff. Goes around town wearing those damned wild dresses and fruitcake hats. She's an embarrassment. Doesn't do anything of substance. Puts on these damned bike and sled races and the like and all the time the school's gone to hell, the state park's a fiasco. The roads are full of potholes – and there's *all* of seven vehicles on the island. Sidewalks are crumbling. One of these fudgies is gonna' trip on a curb and fall flat on his face doing multiple damages or break an ankle in one of those yard-wide cracks in the sidewalk and sue the damned place for millions."

Kirby Kitchen drew a breath and Ira glanced over. The speaker was short, stocky – fireplug like, burly, thick black hair on his arms. Bald with long sideburns – way out of style – with a large brown mustache. Starbursts of hair protruding out his ears – looked like a Turkish wrestler.

"Marquette Park looks like hell. We used to have the most beautiful flower gardens there. All kinds of flowers. Now we got a bunch of godam geraniums. You'd think a woman would know better than that. She lets those ferries – all of them empty their bilges out in Haldimand Bay. Turds are floating out there on any given day. She's sorry. But she walks around in that get up, talks to all the fudgies and the locals. They all think she's the berries. A damned piece of fluff." And he got up and left. Ordered nothing.

Whey don't you tell us what you really think. Well, not every one loves our fair Katy.

"Congratulations," said Fran, "You've now met Mr. Blowhole. That's what we call him around here. Comes in once or twice a month, rarely orders anything other than coffee. Talks to whoever will listen. Like he said – runs for mayor every two years – doesn't have a chance in hell of winning. Runs anyway."

"And his name is Kirby Kitchen? What's his motto, 'Kitchen is Kleen'?"

Kirby Kitchen was not the only character Ira met in September. He was in his office, early, working on some state reports, smoking a cigar that resembled a blacksnake when in his office walked – she walked right by Janet, didn't even look at her – a woman with the brightest, reddest hair he'd ever seen. Even redder than Katy McCormack's. Her skin was as pale as a full moon and everything he could see of her was covered with freckles – even her lips which were as thin as razor blades. He could not tell what fashion her hair was – long – that's all he knew – wild, but not curly – straight. She was tall, rangy – that would be polite for skinny. Nice breasts, though, which stood our firmly in her tight white blouse. It was a riding blouse. He could tell because she was wearing jodhpurs and riding boots. In her right had she held what he guessed was a riding hat – it had a scarf on it. She held a leather crop in her left hand with which she was beating the top of her left boot and it was making a hell of a smack.

Looking like that her name has to be Mary Murphy, Ira thought. *Pure Irish.*

"Look, here," she said hotly, "if you don't do something with those little Freeman creeps I'm going to stick this crop up their little asses. Are you allowed to smoke in here? Isn't there a rule or something?"

Ira had been around too long to be flustered or intimidated, "And who might those little Freeman creeps be?" ignoring the remark about the cigar.

"Let me tell you – if they live long enough you'll know plenty about them. I don't think they'll live to be twenty. They're delinquents," she sputtered.

"That may be, but who are they?"

"They're pissants. Ned and Ted Freeman – twins from hell. Teenagers. Mr. Freeman, and I hate to use the word 'Mr.', runs Freeman's Fudge. And those two little pricks ride up behind you on their bikes – they get right beside you. Each one of the little shits has an air horn – you know one of those canned jobs – and they open them up. There's a law against stuff like that. They do it to everyone and then they run off on their bikes laughing like the idiots they are. Any horse will bolt. Christ, it's as quiet as church most of the time. These horses have never heard noises. They go crazy. The one I was on today, Lady Blue, is skittish anyway and when those fools rode by and let off those horns she reared straight up and it was all I could do to stay in the saddle. Horse went crazy, but when she came down

I took after them, but on those bikes they can make a turn here and one there and Lady Blue cannot."

"And you are?"

"Juliet Steinbrenner."

"Steinbrenner is a famous name."

"My grandfather and Georgie's father were brothers. Georgie's father went into building freighters. Grandfather Charlie went into building sailboats. Made damned good ones, too. Best on the Great Lakes. Then it got hard to find good lumber and rather than cheapen his product he quit making them. Actually, his son, and my Daddy, Charles Junior, was running the company, but Daddy had no say in things. Charlie Senior made all the decisions and when he decided to close the plant Daddy didn't have a job. He got a job selling boats, but that didn't last long. Jumped off Arch Rock just before Grandpa Charlie died. The old man still had a lot of money and to make a long story short I inherited it – only heir. That's why I can afford to fart around and ride these horses. I've got a forty-four foot "Steiny" named "Little Sassy" that I sail when I'm not riding horses. I'm thirty-seven, independent, never been married and don't intend to be. Now, what are you gong to do about those Freeman delinquents?"

"Well, I guess the first thing I'd do would be to walk down to the fudge shop and talk to daddy. I think every parent should have a chance to handle their own kids. Then I'd wait and see what happens after that. Is that good enough? I don't know what the rule is, but I smoke in my office. It's about lunch time I'm going to the Pink Pony. Can I buy you lunch?"

"I think not. I'm not interested in lunch. I'm interested in the Bobbsey Twins. You take care of them and I'll consider lunch, but I don't put out – and the cigars are definitely a no-no."

Why don't you tell me what you really think.

Ira did not fluster easy, but in this instance he did redden – slightly.

"Good, I always like to know how I stand on the first date."

"Goodbye." And she left, tapping the riding crop on her left boot even harder.

Ira finished his report and his cigar. Pondered about the girl. Wondered how he could have been on the island since August and not seen her. With that hair she could be seen a mile away. He went to lunch at the Pink Pony. He tried not to eat lunch out often. Prices were high and forty grand would not go far. Usually he packed his lunch. But it was important to get around. After lunch he stopped at Freeman's Fudge. Mr. Freeman seemed to be rather meek but promised to "speak to the boys". Ira was not going to hold his breath.

He would not have had to hold his breath long. Two days later Juliet Steinbrenner again walked directly past Janet and into his office.

"This is becoming a habit," Ira said, "I do have a secretary out there who shows people in."

"Don't have time for that. And those dumb asses did it again. Your little talk didn't do much good."

Ira hadn't thought it would.

"Here's the law," and she shoved a book of ordinances under his nose. And sure enough you were not allowed to do anything that would frighten the horses on the island – workhorse or otherwise.

"I'll take care of it," he said. He stood, got his helmet and started for the door, "Stay put," he said, and left her standing in the middle of his office. *Damned helmet makes me look like an asshole.*

Ira swung himself easily onto his bike. He was getting used to it, besides he'd lost twenty pounds just from riding the thing and all the walking he had done. Plus he was never full, couldn't afford to eat out, and was too lazy to cook much. Did some stuff in the microwave. It was a short ride to the school. Walked into the principal's office and asked to see the Freeman twins.

"Your bikes out there?" he asked when they arrived and nodded toward the bike racks full of bikes, "Yes," they answered.

"Principal Fuller, I need to borrow these two boys for a very short time. They'll be back in time for their next class. C'mon boys, we're goin' for a quick ride."

Ira walked the boys to the bike racks. Their bikes were as identical as they were. Black, sleek racing bikes – looked as if they had a hundred gears. No wonder Juliet could not catch them on Lady Blue.

"Unlock 'em and get on 'em. We're goin' for a short ride," Ira commanded.

"Whaddaya, want with us?" one of them asked. He didn't know which one as he could not tell one from the other.

"You'll see, follow me," and took off, heading for the police station. When he was out of sight of the school, he stopped,

"Pull over," he commanded. They did.

"Gentlemen," Ira started, "I've got a deal for you. It's this. You quit scaring the local equestrian group. You know who I mean? That's people who ride horses and that's damned near everybody on the island – that is those who don't ride bikes. You quit scaring the horse riders and I'll pretend this never happened. You scare one more rider and I'll throw your little butts in jail and I guarantee you you'll be there for a week – because I will find something to keep you in there that long. Now, we will all ride to the jail so you can get a good look at it and you will apologize to a Miss Steinbrenner. Do you know who she is?"

"No," they answered in unison.

"Well, you soon will and you'll not forget her as her hair is as red as your faces. Let's go."

Off they went, Ira riding slowly so the boys would have time to think about it.

Juliet Steinbrenner was not only there but standing in the same spot – tapping her riding crop on the top of her left riding boot.

"Miss Steinbrenner, meet the Freeman twins Ned and Ted. They came to look at one of our jail cells," and he led them towards one, unlocked it and kind of herded them inside. "Have a seat." Only there were no chairs. Just an upper and lower bunk, a toilet and a wash basin. "That's okay, just sit on the bunk. Miss Steinbrenner, would you please come in here a second. The boys have something to say."

Juliet walked to the cell door still tapping the riding crop on her boot.

"Go ahead, boys."

Both of them had their head down looking at their feet.

"We're sorry, we didn't mean anything by it," one of them said.

"Yeah, we were just having fun," chimed the other.

"Well, your having fun was not fun for me or anyone else you've scared. Only a very skilled rider can stay on a horse when she rears or bolts. You could have killed someone."

"We're sorry," they said in unison.

"And I believe they are and I don't think they will bother you any more," Ira stated. "Okay, you two ride back to school. I'm going to call Mr. Fuller in five minutes and you two'd best be in your next classroom. Now go."

Never had Ira seen two boys move so quickly.

"Now, how about lunch?"

"No cigars!"

They walked to the Mustang Lounge. This was going to be his dinner. He ordered a cup of clam chowder and shish kabob that featured beef, shrimp, green peppers, onions and mushrooms – accompanied by a garden salad. She ordered a bowl of clam chowder and extra rolls. Also, an Amstel that Ira drooled over, since he was on duty.

They small talked. Ira stayed away from anything that might be contentious. He asked her about Grandfather Charlie and his sailboat business – how he got started, where it took place, when he died and the like. He asked her about her boat and found that she was in love with the sea – well it would be the lakes – more so than even horses. She sailed whenever she could, even in rough weather, she was a risk taker. She competed in the annual race from Chicago to Mackinac – finished third in her class, once. Was out to win it. Graduated from Stevens College in Missouri. Had a degree in journalism – never used it. Never officially worked. Didn't have to – she inherited seven million dollars when she turned twenty-one. The boat business had been good to Grandfather Charlie. No one could say Grandfather Charlie was not successful. Perhaps not as successful as Georgie's, father, but he did okay. She kept busy with her horses and boat.

Then she said something that surprised him – shocked him,

"I've had fourteen romance novels published under the name of Della Queen. Made some money on my own."

"I'll be damned," he said genuinely impressed, "I didn't think you were romantically inclined."

"It's a lot easier to write about it than live it. I've tried both. Believe me, writing is easier."

They talked on, but he was adamant about taking only an hour for lunch,

"Got to go," he said, "I'm on the taxpayer's time. How about a ride tonight?" he reddened and stammered, "With a horse I mean." Realized what he'd said and reddened even more, "*On* a horse! I'm not good, but I'd like to go around the island. I'll stop at Cindy's and rent one."

"You're blushing. Yes, I'd like that. With you around I won't have to worry about the Freeman brats. Don't worry about a horse. Come to my place after work and I'll have one saddled up for you. Red is about as nice a horse as you will find on the island and he's big like you. You'll like him."

"I don't have the slightest idea where you live."

"Live on Trillium. It's a dead end. Last house. Can't miss it. It's a big son-of-a-bitch. Stables out back. We'll take the back way. What time?"

"Well, I'm on duty 'til six. This is dinner for me. So, I'll come on over after work. I'll be in uniform. That okay?"

"Like I said, it will keep the Freeman brats at bay."

"I really don't think you'll have to worry about the Freeman boys anymore."

She was correct the place was big, but so were the rest up there. I say "up" for Trillium was at the top of Great Turtle Park hill. She had three acres – mostly up, but enough level so that she had a nice stable and a separate tack barn behind the house. Two huge Great Danes announced his arrival. They took turns smelling his crotch, until Juliet came out the front door and called them.

"Acey! Deucey! Leave the man alone. Come here, damnit." And they did and cowered by her side, "Get back in back!" and they did. He had to pass them as they went to the stables, but they were gnawing on some bones – cracking them like matchsticks. They didn't even look up, but he looked at them. Acey was the male, brindle in color, powerful; he stood thirty-two inches at the shoulder. Deucey, the female, was more graceful but still very powerful – fawn in color and thirty inches at the shoulder – large for a female.

Red proved to be a beautiful horse – roan, seventeen hands. She was correct, Red was big. They picked up Lost Bear Trail a few hundred yards behind her house, then up Garrison Road to Four Corners, took Crooked Tree Road until it turned south and then rode directly to Lake Shore. The horses ambled.

On Lake Shore they rode side by side. Juliet's Lady Blue wanted to run, but she held him back. Red was content to just make his way. They talked. She'd had a much older brother, David. They called him Sonny. He was born before the polio vaccine had been discovered. Caught polio and before they could figure it out he'd died. Charlie Junior nearly lost his mind. Her parents waited sixteen years before they decided to have another child. Her mother was forty-two when Juliet was born. Had a bad heart and died when Juliet was four. Juliet remembered her only as an odor, just her perfume, could not remember her face at all. The death of his son and wife were the final nails in Charlie Junior's coffin and he jumped off the Arch Rock during Juliet's freshman year at Stevens.

"I'm going to win that race," she stated.

"What race?" he asked, innocently.

"There's only one race," she snapped, "The race from Chicago to Mackinac. Should have won a couple of years ago when I finished third. I've got the best boat – just not the best crew."

"That's tough," he said sympathetically and not sarcastically.

"More than that, it's exasperating. You need muscle on that trip."

"Uh, huh."

"You'd do good."

"Do good, what?"

"Do good in the race."

Ira didn't really know what to say. He wasn't certain he knew what she had said – what she was talking about.

"What do you mean?"

"I mean you'd do good in the race. You're just the kind of guy I'm looking for."

"Are you crazy? What the hell are you talking about? I don't know a damn thing about sailing. I've never even been on a sailboat," he stammered and blurted at the same time.

"That's good, you won't be telling me how to do my job. I don't need skill, I need muscle," she stated, "I'll teach you all you need to know. Do you get sea sick?"

"Sea sick? How the hell do I know. The longest I've been on a boat is Arnold's Ferry. You must be losing your marbles. I'm a cop. When your race is going on I'll be keeping law and order on this island."

"Aw, it's only a couple of days. I'm certain the island will be safe in Officers Dickerson's and Upland's hands."

"When is this thing?"

"Always the same time of year – the third week in July."

"Well, I won't even have any vacation time by then."

"Don't worry; I'm a very good friend of Katy's. We're both red heads – did you notice."

"Well that would be awful hard to miss now, wouldn't it? Look, I'm not interested in racing a damn boat," and he took out a Roi Tan that looked like it had been tarred. Just as he started to light it Red took off like a shot. Ira had both hands off the reins and he fell back, kind of like being hit from behind in a car. He wasn't unseated but he had a look of frantic on his face. His cigar went over his left shoulder and his old Zippo clattered to the asphalt. He grabbed at the reins and pulled hard. Red came to a stop. Juliet rode up behind, laughing,

"I should have told you old Red doesn't like anything that resembles fire. I never thought you'd be dumb enough to light a cigar."

"Well, after what you just proposed, a cigar was in order and a stiff drink. What's old Red's take on whiskey?"

She laughed, "Never tried it. I guess if you brought some for old Red he'd not object." And laughed again, more of a snicker as if she could visualize it.

"Well, think it over," she said.

"I don't have to think it over – I'm not going to do it. Let's talk about something else – like where are all the drugs coming from that hit this place? There's a bunch."

She admitted there was a drug problem, been that way for several years, but she had no idea where they were coming from.

They rode in silence for several minutes – many minutes. There did not seem much to say. Juliet kept steady pressure on Lady Blue's rein and Red just plodded along. They took Annex Road back to her house. They dismounted and walked the horses to the stable.

"Do you need some help?" he asked almost apologetically.

"No, that's okay. I can take care of them okay. Thanks, though."

He hesitated, "Say, I'm sorry about how I said it but I don't know anything about boats. I'm from Ohio. You've got the wrong guy. There must be a hundred guys on this island that know what they're doing."

"That's so, but most of them are my competitors. And the ones that are left over – I wouldn't have. I shouldn't have asked – I don't even know you, but I know what it takes to win."

"Never hurts to ask. Listen, I enjoyed most of this. Would you like to do it again – sometime?"

"As you said – it never hurts to ask."

Ira rode back to Darlene's. She was nursing a beer, an Amstel, and chain smoking – as usual,

"Have a nice ride?"

"God! News travels fast."

"It is an island – small. Want a beer?"

"Too true," he'd heard that in an Australian movie.

She popped one and placed it before him, "Glass?"

"No, this is fine," he took a long drink – he was dry from talk and embarrassment or whatever it was he felt. Lit a Roi Tan.

"What do you know about Juliet Steinbrenner?"

"She a suspect?"

"You know what I mean. What kind of person is she?"

"Top drawer. Good lady. Helps the poor. Doesn't lord her money. Is kind to animals. Minds her own business. Is one hell of a sailor and a pretty good horsewoman. I think, lonely. Won't let anyone get too close. Several have tried. The fact that she had lunch with you today and went riding with you will be the talk of the town. Still feels the loss of her dad, and a mother and brother she never knew. Loved her grandfather – took care of him to the end. More bark than bite. Someone you'd like."

"You knew about lunch?"

"And so does the rest of the island."

They turned to other subjects. He liked Darlene and she him. She'd given him the big room as soon as the last tenant left. She fixed them each a BLT. She could nurse a beer, but she offered him two more as they talked and he went through two Roi Tans. It was dark when they finished. He went to his room and lay on the bed without undressing. He thought of Juliet. Juliet as in Romeo and Juliet – he thought. He was no Romeo that was for certain, and she no Fair Juliet.

But there was something that attracted him – her independent air – yet she was vulnerable – that was certain. Her looks? He could not quite define how he felt, but he liked her looks, her freckles, her blazing hair, just about everything – yet many people thought her plain – at most.

He heard nothing from her. Obviously he had discouraged the Freeman twins. September made way for October. There was not a leaf left by mid-month and it had snowed twice by Halloween. On Beggars' Night it was so cold the kids had to put their costumes over snow suits. Things were very quiet. The drug business seemed to be drying up. It was too damned cold for the kids to get together to use them. He had caught a couple of eighteen year old senior boys smoking pot,

"Look," he said, "Do you know the penalty for smoking pot? It's a felony. Do you really want that record to follow you? You, know I could bust you right now. Jeeze, how dumb can you be. You can smell pot a mile away. Where'd you get it?"

"Dunno," one answered, shrugging his shoulders.

"Look, I don't think you understand what I can do here. Now where'd you get it?"

"We bought it off a fudgie last summer."

"And you're just now using it?"

"Yeah, we were afraid."

"That's good and I hope you're afraid to do it again. Everybody gets one chance. Turn your pockets out." There was no more.

Kirby Kitchen starting campaigning the first of October and was in high gear by the fifteenth. He had signs all over the island. He bought some time on WMAK and accused Katy McCormack of sleeping through the past thirty-four years. He referred to her once as Rip Van McCormack. There was no League of Women Voters on the island so no formal debates were ever set up. She refused to debate him so he'd have rallies at different place. A handful of people would show up. Kirby could get nasty. Wondered why "Kathyrn" never married. Would a real woman dress like that? What was she trying to prove? When would the first horse break a leg in one of the pot holes on Huron Street? Could we get some real flowers in Marquette Park?

Weather-wise election day can be a bitch on Mackinac. This particular day was no exception. It was snowing hard when Ira awoke. He stuck an onion bagel in the microwave and smothered it with peanut butter. He was still learning how to use Darlene's coffee maker, but what he made wasn't bad. Had two cups. Walked to the station. Janet was there,

"Mornin', Chief. You've got snow on your head. Where's your hat?"

"Left it here," he said, shaking water and snow both from his shaggy gray hair. He needed a hair cut.

"Don't you have a hat at home?"

"I don't have anything at home."

"Well, you best go down to Reynolds and get a toboggan. You're going to need it."

Reynolds passed for what was the department store on the island.

"I don't need a sled."

"Silly, you wear a toboggan."

Ira was puzzled and showed it.

"Up here a toboggan is a warm wool hat – you know that!"

"No", he replied, "I've never heard that."

"Flatland furriner. Get one anyway. Your uniform hat is not going to do it."

"Katy said I'm supposed to guard the precincts today so there's no fraud. We may not even have a voter – let alone fraud."

There were only two voting precincts on the island and one of them was wasted – there was need but for one. And that would be on any election day and especially this one, for the turnout was light – and that was putting it mildly.

Nevertheless, Ira walked to the school and stood around for a while as a few diehard voters walked or came on horse. Most of them came to get out of the cold. While he was there thirty-eight people voted. After a while he walked over to Saint Anne's Catholic Church where the other precinct was located. While he was there Jack and Mary Walsh from the Mohawk walked over and voted,

"How you gettin' along at Darlene's?" Jack inquired, "With her cigarettes and your cigars I'll bet that place smells like a Chinese opium den."

"We're fine," he replied, "Did you vote for Kitchen?"

"None of your damn business. It's a secret ballot, you know."

"I voted for him," chimed Mary, "I didn't want him to get skunked."

And he nearly did. Only one-hundred thirty-one voters walked, rode horses, snow shoed or slid to the polls. Kirby Kitchen received twenty-four of their votes.

Kirby couldn't give a concession speech. He was busy embalming Gertrude Macbeth. She had died on the way to the polls. "Lady Macbeth" the islanders called her but not to her face. She was a spinster who lived in one of the West Bluff cottages. She'd been on the way to the school to vote. She was bundled up like Randy in *The Christmas Story*. She had a heart attack. Doc Prendergast (yes, of that famous family) said she was dead before she hit the snow. Kirby was just injecting the embalming fluid when Ira walked in,

"Tell them I said, 'I'll win yet'. Can you imagine there are only two dozen intelligent people on this whole damn island."

CHAPTER EIGHT

Indian summer is so called because that was the time of year the Native Americans harvested their crops. It comes to Mackinac Island every year – some more glorious than others. This one was glorious. There was not a leaf hanging anywhere and the naked trees looked like hands praying to a native god. The days were in the sixties – on Saturday it got to seventy-one, almost a record. If it lasted a week people were happy. It went on for ten days. On the second Saturday Juliet Steinbrenner walked into Ira's office – Janet was off duty. He had not seen her since they took the ride around the island. Ira was looking at some "Wanted" posters. Contrary to what people might think, Mackinac was just the place such people might head for. Except this would be a mighty dumb time to do it for everyone on the island would notice a stranger so Ira was not looking too hard. Nevertheless, she came in so quietly he did not know she was there and when she said, "Hi, there" he was so startled he dropped everything he was holding.

"Dammit, girl, don't do that!"

She was wearing tight jeans, a loose plaid flannel shirt, boots with heels and a blue bandanna, the way women wear them – not the way men do.

"Sorry. I was wondering if you'd like to take a ride on the Little Sassy. I'll have to take her out of the water next week. This'll be the last time I'll be able to take her out."

"I'm on duty until six. It's dark by then."

"I don't mean today. I was talking about tomorrow. You have to work tomorrow?"

"No, I'm off. Upland's on duty. I'm not gonna' change my mind."

"Who said anything about changing your mind? I'm asking you to go on a boat ride – the last one of the season," she reddened – almost to the color of her hair. "I'll buy lunch – but if you'd rather not ......" and her words trailed off.

"No," he said quickly, seeing her distress. *This is hard for her,* he thought. "I'd like to go. Where and when?"

"I keep her at the British Landing state docks. Early, before the wind really kicks up. It will be plenty windy. Ten o'clock. Dress warm. No cigars."

He thought about driving the patrol car there, but then he thought better, *As soon as I do, something will happen and Upland will need it.* Instead he took the cop bike. He was getting used to it – actually he was rounding into shape – the kind of shape he should have been in all along. He locked it in the bike rack – wouldn't do to have the cop bike stolen. He'd dressed warmly. Had on Levi's, T-shirt under a sweatshirt with a hood, wool socks, boots and had stopped at Reynolds and purchased a navy blue toboggan.

Ira was correct when he had said he knew nothing about sail boats. He did not. But even *he* knew the Little Sassy was special. She shone. Her hull, made of solid oak, gleamed with varnish. You couldn't see a single knot in the wood. Charlie Steinbrenner had made her himself. That's not to say his company built the boat. He built it. Took him over three years. Only sailed on her a few times as his health was failing. Her brass and all the other bright work shone. Her teak and mahogany trim was oiled and deep in color. Her mast of solid oak was as straight as a soldier's back and her pennant snapped sharply in the breeze. And there was a breeze, a good one. Juliet had been correct – it was windy and it was not yet ten. He thought she would be correct, also, about it being windier later. But the morning was brilliant. Not a cloud, anywhere, and the sun as bright as a newly minted twenty-dollar gold piece. She hailed him from the stern,

"Ah, the new deck hand! Oops! I should say, the rookie. Come around on the dock and come aboard. She's drawn up close."

She was wearing blue deck pants, white deck shoes – no socks, a white turtleneck that contrasted with her flaming hair which was being blown all ways. She wore a grey hooded sweatshirt – unzipped and the hood laid back. She was working with some ropes – lines, as Ira later learned they were called.

She was a ketch and large enough to have a gangway. Ira crossed it easily and stepped aboard the Little Sassy. *Apropos name*, he thought. Juliet was still at the stern fussing with the same line. He walked back,

"I don't know anything about it, but can I help?"

"Nope. Thanks. I use this to tie down the tarp that goes over the dinghy. Somehow it got tangled up. That's not like me I usually have my lines coiled and neat."

He watched.

After that she did everything that was needed to get them under weigh. She raised the mainsail herself. The wind caught the Little Sassy and pushed her quickly out into Maniboajo Bay. She stood at the wheel, hood still down – red hair flying. He stood behind. He had read enough of the Iliad to conjure up the Sirens and he thought one of them might have looked like Juliet.

It was just past ten and the wind had picked up from the time he had locked the bike. The wind blew them south at a more than fair clip – they were flying. Spray came over the bow and while it did not soak them it hit their faces and stung. Within a few minutes they sighted Bois Blanc Island and once they got the island between the boat and the wind the wind lessened and the boat slowed considerably. As they rounded Bois Blanc and headed north they were against the wind and Juliet tacked or whatever you do in that situation – Ira did not know – but she did it. And there was time for her to explain what the jib was, the main mast, the mizzen, the mizzenmast, port and starboard (he knew that, but kept his mouth shut), fore and aft, the beam, the freeboard, the gunnels, the stern and bow (he rolled his eyes here – did she think he was an idiot). On and on. They sailed north until they spotted Mackinac Island, sailed around the east side and back to where they had started but instead of docking Juliet headed west to St. Ignace and docked. He offered help but she and the harbor master tied her up neat in a matter of minutes. He was wet – a little, and cold – a lot. She still had not zipped up her sweatshirt – no hood, either.

"The Crab Pot has great food," she said and led him to it. It was near, on the dock. An old place, worn, with lots of charm. Only locals were there at the time of year. They sat by the window – it was open.

"The view's nice. I've seen a lot of water today and I'm cold." He closed the window.

"Wimp."

"Let's compromise. I'll open the window – and then light up a cigar."

"No cigar."

"Wimp."

They looked at the menu – paper – worn and stain covered. He supposed they'd order new ones for next season. They wouldn't be open much longer. In fact a sign said they closed on the fifteenth.

"What would you like? Remember I said I was buying," this was Juliet speaking.

"Hot. Black. Coffee! And lots of it." His teeth were chattering.

"Men, the weaker sex."

"Hey, I happen to know you ladies are wrapped in fat. Adipose. Gives you curves and keeps you warm. However, you don't look like you've got a hell of a lot."

"You've got my share," and she looked at his belly.

Truth was he'd lost twenty pounds and thought he was pretty trim. It embarrassed him a little. He didn't like people to think he was out of shape.

"I'm working at it," and it was more of a mumble.

He did order black coffee, also the fresh-perch basket. The perch was deep fried and came with a heap of greasy fries and cole slaw.

"You're right. The food's great."

"No cholesterol there. Should help you lose weight."

He was further embarrassed. Almost came back with a smart-alecky remark, but decided to hold his tongue. She was not the enemy.

She ordered chamomile tea, a dozen shrimp to peel and a side salad.

"Lot's of crackers," she said.

After lunch and two mugs of black coffee Ira asked, "Want a beer?"

"I'm driving."

"I'd have one but I think the benefit from the alcohol would be offset by the cold."

They dawdled awhile. She paid. They left.

The way back was even colder for the wind, as Juliet predicted, picked up considerably and the sun had gone behind clouds that hadn't existed before lunch. Mercifully it was only a run of six miles. But Ira was frozen by the time they docked. Juliet had managed to zip up her sweatshirt – no hood.

Juliet fooled around with all the things that had to be done before they left. He helped as she instructed. Moving around on deck warmed him a little – enough that he began to appreciate the trip.

"I had fun," he admitted, "Thanks for lunch."

"We'll do it again. In the spring when it's warmer, although it can be cool in the spring," and she reached up and kissed him on the cheek. Her lips were cold but warmer than his face. Then his face seemed to be warm all over.

He walked to the bike rack. The cop bike was gone.

CHAPTER NINE

"Someone stole my damn bike," he was pissed and incredulous at the same time. "Someone's got a lot of damn nerve! That's one thick cable. Someone worked a long time on that baby." He suspected the Freeman twins, but said nothing.

Juliet, who had been several steps behind him, quickened her pace and was beside him. She kind of snickered.

"It's not funny, damn it."

"I know it," and she straightened her face, "But it is ironic." She had a hard time to keep from laughing, "C'mon, Lady Blue can carry us both."

"I'll walk, damn it. Or call Upland," but then he didn't have his cell phone and she never carried one.

"Don't be silly."

Lady Blue was still tied up. At least no one had stolen *her*. But then the penalty for horse-thieving was much greater than for bike-thieving.

Have you ever seen two people trying to get on a horse at the same time? Mack Sennett time. She couldn't get on until he got on. Once mounted he had to slide his considerable butt over the hind-bow of the saddle. Not easy for a nearing fifty year old two-hundred twenty pounder. And once back there where do you put your feet? His kind of hung out – some – for the ass-end of Lady Blue was considerable even given the fact she was a mare.

Juliet mounted with a lot less trouble,

"Gidyap"

And Lady Blue did – and Lady Blue did at a trot and they just about lost Ira. He started to go backward – heels over head.

"Jesus Christ!" he bellowed and grabbed at anything he could. What he got was a handful of Juliet's blue deck pants at her left hip and all of her right breast.

"Let go, you idiot!"

But he did not – at least until he had gained control of his body and then he slipped his hands down to and gripped both her thighs.

"Put your arms around my waist," she ordered.

"Why didn't you warn me! You could have killed me."

She didn't have an answer. It had been a dumb thing to do. They rode in complete silence. Lady Blue labored. She was a mare and small – beautiful, though. Though they were silent Ira was not unhappy to have his hands around her waist. Her small breasts met the top of his clasped hands. They moved with the movement of the saddle. He was surprised at how ample her waist was. *There's more to this girl than meets the eye.*

It was a long ride back, but not another word passed between them, until they reached Four Corners.

"Take me back to the station. I want to file a report on my bike,"

She didn't answer but went that way.

Getting off was nearly as bad as getting on. Juliet had to swing her right leg over Lady Blue's mane and kind of jump down. Ira struggled to get over the hind-bow then dismounted in the usual fashion. None of it was pretty.

"Sorry," she said and meant it. He did not reply.

There in the rack was his bike – a note was attached to the seat. He walked to it and read the note:

Thought your relationship might need a nudge.

It didn't work, you dumb ass, whoever you are!

He lit a cigar, fuming in at least two ways, and trudged to Darlene's.

Monday morning Ira was at the station early – with one thing on his mind – to find out who took his bike. When Janet came in he asked her to write in longhand "Mary had a little lamb. Its fleece was white as snow."

"Why?" she asked.

"It's a detective game."

She did. It was close, but it did not match.

Ed Dickerson came it at six for the night shift,

"Mind writing out something for me?"

"I guess not."

His did not match either.

He had to wait two shifts before Doug Upland came in,

"Doug, I'd like you to write something for me."

When Ira told him what it was he replied,

"A nursery rhyme. Are you losing it?"

"I've got my reasons."

Doug Upland had never learned to write cursive. His teachers didn't think it was important. His looked as if written by a kindergartner. Obviously he did not write the note.

Only five people had keys to the bike lock and all other such locks. On Wednesday he called Mayor McCormack's secretary and made an appointment. Her office was just across the street,

"To what do I owe this honor, Chief?" Katy asked. "I usually have to come and see you. I think, in fact, this is the first time you've been in my office since you hired on."

"I don't know. Someone stole my bike at British Landing on Sunday and when I got back to the office it was in the rack – with a note on the seat. I've got the note here,"and he produced it – laid it on her desk. "Only five people have a key to that lock. I didn't write the note and neither did three other people."

"How do you know?"

"I checked their handwriting – I am the chief of police – remember – and a PI for twenty years. Theirs didn't match. I'm here to get a sample of yours."

"What if I refuse."

"I resign."

"No need for either. I wrote it. I took the bike, too."

"That was a dumb-assed thing to do. I nearly got killed on that horse."

"I was just trying to help things along. Juliet's a friend of mine, a good friend. She's a number one lady. Has always needed a good man in her life. I did it for her – not you. I think you're a good man."

Ira was quiet for a good while. He'd long ago learned to think before he spoke. He wanted to let her know how he felt, but keep her on his side, also.

"Well, regardless of your motive it was still a dumb-ass thing to do. Everyone on this island loves you, except of course for Kirby Kitchen and he's just frustrated. I'm certain Miss Steinbrenner can handle her own affairs and I know I can. Juliet's a nice lady – that's all I can say. We had a great time Sunday – that is until some .... some ...... busybody took my bike. This person did more harm than good, as Juliet and I did not part on good terms. Did you ever see the film *The Ringer*?"

"No. Why?"

"Well, in this movie Paul Newman plays a kind of town ner-do-well, a guy they call Sully, but it turns out that a lot of people in this small town are dependent on him – including his landlady Miss Beryl, played by Jessica Tandy. Miss Beryl was once his eighth grade teacher. Sully has an old piece of property, his childhood home, where he grew up. His dad was an alcoholic and beat his mother around so he has bad memories about the place and lets it fall into disrepair and doesn't pay the taxes. He's about to lose the house, but he doesn't give a good damn. Miss Beryl pays the taxes on it. Sully is really pissed but he's warned by his best friend that if he does not accept it, his best friend will quit being his friend – forever-ever. So, it's at the end of the movie – it's late at night. Sully comes home tired out from things. Miss Beryl asks him if he wants a cup of tea. She's been asking him this for years and he says, 'Not now. Not ever.' This is what he's been saying for years and then he asks, 'Why do you keep asking me?' and she says, 'Other people change their minds occasionally. I keep thinking you might.' Then he says, 'There's a rumor going around that you did a good deed. Stuck your nose where it didn't belong' and she replies, 'I know it. I'm an old woman and I'm entitled'. He doesn't say anything for a minute or two and then says, 'Well, you're forgiven.' And she says, 'Thank you.' Well, Mayor, that's about where you and I stand."

And he left.

CHAPTER TEN

Winter came. Mountains of snow, tons of sleet, winds whipping, power lines down, trees snapped. Just damned cold.

Jesse Parker who owned the local hardware said,

"Worse winter since `50."

India Ivory, much younger stated,

"Worse winter since `77."

Depends on when you were born.

Christmas came and went. Ira and Juliet avoided each other. Locals enjoyed winter activities. Katy McCormack organized several sleigh rides and races. Those were run on good days. A good day was when the wind was not howling and snow was not coming down horizontally. But these are hearty people.

Islanders saved their old Christmas trees for the "Ice Bridge". That being the name for when the lake froze over and one could walk from the island to St. Ignace. By late January the lake was frozen between the two towns. Though to make certain, Sam Bradford and George Rangle each took a twenty pound chipping bar and tested the thickness. Eleven inches. They did this the entire way. The path zigzagged according to the thickness of the ice. Sam and George marked the way with red flags. Upon their return with the news that the ice was safe the islanders took their discarded Christmas trees and made a lane all the way to St. Ignace. Then others would mark some of the trees with reflector tape so it would show up at night when a flashlight was shown upon it. The custom of walking across the ice bridge was initiated by the attorneys at Herrinton, Menezes and Smathers, but over the years most of the islanders had participated in the affair. The "bridge" lasted from two days to two months. This winter there was no need to hurry the walk. The round trip into St. Ignace itself and back was approximately thirteen miles. Of course some people used snowmobiles – but many islanders thought that was cheating.

One of the highlights of the winter is a home and home basketball game between the Mackinac Island Lakers and the St. Ignace Saints. On a designated Friday night the Lakers, along with their coaches, cheerleaders, and fans, walk across the ice bridge and play a basketball game. The next night, Saturday, the St. Ignace team returns the favor.

Ira thought about it – thought about asking Juliet if she wanted to go for a walk – outdoor type that she was. He'd thought about her every day. Couldn't get her off his mind. Kind of like Willie Nelson's song.

On Thursday before the game he called,

"It's short notice, I know, but I thought you might want to go for a walk."

"Who is this?"

He was chagrined, to say the least. He'd forgotten to identify himself and she had forgotten his voice.

"It's Ira, your cavalry man."

She laughed, "I'd about given up on you. I really was sorry. I know who took your bike."

"I do, too. Let's not talk about it, okay."

"Okay."

"I wondered if you might want to go for a walk Friday night. I'm off duty."

"Outside? It's cold. Maybe. Where to?"

"Yes, outside. You froze me on that boat of yours. It's my turn. Meet me at Perrot Point at five."

"If you want me, come get me. Are we going to walk the Ice Bridge?"

"Dress warm. I'll be there at four-thirty."

It was cold – very cold, but the day had been brilliant – sunny not a cloud the whole day – not one. No snow for a couple of days. It gets dark early in January. It was dusk when Ira arrived at Juliet's house. It wasn't too cold for Acey and Deucey to start barking as he approached. Fortunately they were chained up in the back. They had a heated house and were snug in it but came roaring out of it and strained at their leashes so that they stood on their back legs just aching to get at him – it seemed. Juliet opened the back door and yelled at them, locked it and walked around to the side. She was dressed warmly including a parka she'd got from a friend who'd served in the Air Force in Alaska. She also wore a pair of warm boots. Ira had a pair of coveralls on over his uniform. For some reason he just felt it might be well if he was in uniform. He wore his toboggan and gloves.

They walked to Perrot Point. There had to be fifty people there: the team, cheerleaders, parents, fans and three members of the band – two drummers and a cymbal player.

"What's all this?" she asked and she was not happy.

"It's the walk for the annual St. Ignace basketball game."

"We're going to walk the Ice Bridge to go to a basketball game! I haven't been to a basketball game since I was in high school."

"C'm'on, it'll be fun. Get outside. Support the team."

"Jesus."

But she went.

All the way the two drummers beat a cadence like the drummer boys in the Civil War. It was slow and you could walk to it – some stayed pretty much in step. The cymbal player clanged accordingly. Most, like Ira and Juliet, just walked. Ira carried a powerful flashlight he occasionally used to shine on the reflectors to help keep them between the trees.

On shore the team was met by their opponents. They walked together to the Saints gym a little over a mile away. Most of the players on both teams knew each other well. At the gym the Saints hosted all the islanders to a hot-dish dinner and a five gallon container of hot chocolate. A five mile walk in ten-degree temperature works up and appetite and both Ira and Juliet devoured their supper and relished the hot chocolate. After they cleared out the tables and chairs the game began. It was really no contest as the St. Ignace team was far superior to the island team. There were thirty-four students in the high school that year and the Lakers had to play an eighth grader. The final score was 74-47 – just reversed the numbers. Ned and Ted Freeman each scored sixteen points in the loss – identical to the end. At the end of the third quarter the custodian lit a huge bonfire that was just right for roasting hotdogs and marshmallows after the game.

S'mores were made and relished. Drinks were hot or cold cider, most took it mulled.

It was after ten when the group departed. Before leaving, both teams stood on the dock and sang their respective alma maters. No one took their hat off. It was colder going back. A couple of degrees below zero. The snow crunched like Corn Flakes. The stars were so brilliant if one had a step ladder he could have picked a bushel full. They gave off such light that it was not necessary to use the flashlight. The drummers did not drum.

She was the one who initiated it,

"My hand's freezing," she said as she pulled off her glove and placed hers inside his large mitten. It was awkward, but pleasant, and they walked that way all the way to the island.

He walked her home, their breath a degree or two from ice crystals. She had her hood drawn tight so he could barely see her face. The outside light was on and it was so cold everything had halos around it, including her hood. He fumbled but was able to pull the string undoing it and pushed the hood back. He drew her near and kissed her full on the mouth. It was quick. She moved her lips to his and kissed him long and lingering,

"I had fun even if we did lose."

"St. Ignace returns the favor tomorrow night. Want to go? We won't have so far to walk."

"Yes, I'd like that. Get that old community spirit."

They walked hand in hand to the Saturday night game – bundled up – for it was still very cold. Ira did not wear his uniform. He wanted to be a spectator, not a policeman. They did not take part in the early festivities; rather they walked in just before tip off. They bought popcorn.

Clearly the Lakers were undermanned but they played a stalling game. It was eight to six at halftime – Saints. In spite of the earlier team meals and feeling of good will there was a fair amount of booing from the Saints' side. In the third quarter each team scored a basket: ten to eight. It was ten to eight with a little under two minutes to go when the Lakers quit stalling and went for the basket. The Freeman twins played guards and Ned drilled a fifteen footer to tie the game. St. Ignace came down, hurried a shot and missed. Ned rebounded and fired a pass to the streaking Ted who laid it in for two and was fouled. He made the foul and all of a sudden the underdog Lakers led by three. There were forty-eight seconds left. Biff Barker, St. Ignace's all-league pivot who was six-three and two-hundred twelve pounds, bulled his way inside. The Lakers scattered as he came barreling in and he had an easy two. Thirty seconds and counting. Ned took it out and passed it in to Ted. Ted brought the ball up the floor with "Boots" Reddig hounding him the whole way. Ted dribbled in circles with Boots and Jerry Wright, the other Saints' guard, on him tight. They were down to fifteen seconds when the Saints Coach yelled for his team to foul. They did. Both the Freeman boys were dead foul shooters. It was a one-shot foul and Ned drilled it. The Saints brought the ball down in a hurry, passed into big Biff. No one on the Lakers could handle him and he just wheeled for the basket and it was a tie game – fourteen to fourteen. Ten seconds.

Ned passed into Ted who drove up the floor with Boots on him like duct tape. Ted is short and Boots, too. With a second and a half on the clock Ted launched an eighteen-footer, a three pointer, which touched nothing but the cords and the Lakers won seventeen to fourteen. Pandemonium on one side – dejection on the other.

Both Ira and Juliet jumped up cheering, popcorn went all over. Juliet caught herself and quickly sat down,

"I don't know why I did that. I don't even like the damned game – and those Freeman boys. Yuck."

"They may not be as bad as we think they are. Pranksters, yes. Vicious, no. They may amount to something after all. Let's see what they look like when they're twenty."

"They'll never live to see twenty."

She was probably correct, but Ira had seen plenty of boys like the Freeman twins make a one-eighty when they got into college or joined the service or just turned twenty-one. He reached over and took her hand. She did not resist, nor did they speak. Silence all the way to her house. He wondered about the dogs, but they were quiet.

She took off her gloves to find her house key – fumbled awhile – found the key, stepped toward the door. Slipped down her hood. Again the outside light and freezing temperatures formed a halo over the light and Juliet's head. A red-haired angel.

"Do you want to come in?"

"Sure."

"No cigars."

"My cigar's frozen."

She unlocked the door and stepped in, he followed. It was the mud room – cold. She took off her coat, slipped off her snowy boots. He did the same, except his boots did not slip off, he tugged. The floor, vinyl tile, was frigid. Another door led to the foyer. It was locked, also. His feet were freezing. He guessed hers were as well. The same key fit both locks. It did not take her long to open the door and Ira was glad. Beyond the foyer was the living room with pile so thick he nearly sank to his ankles. Polar Bear white. No wonder she had taken off her shoes. A dim light inside a ship's lantern cast eerie shadows on the walls. The ceiling was not high. Islanders, not even rich ones, were into eighteen-foot ceiling. Wasted too much heat. What good is heat at the ceilings if the floor is cold? At the far end, and it was a good sized room, was a massive fieldstone fireplace that covered the wall, except for a door that opened into the den. She took him through that door. This room was smaller than the living room – intimate, but with a much higher ceiling. Again, a ship's lantern with a dim light – no – there were two lanterns. The floor was oak and oiled, dull. A large, thick, white, throw rug nestled up to the hearth – back far enough to escape sparks. The fireplace opened into both rooms. As fieldstone had covered the wall in the living room cherry paneling surrounded the fireplace in the den. Three large portraits hung over the mantel, two men and a woman. Ira surmised they were of her father, mother and grandfather.

A low coffee table, large, was centered on the rug. A large and tan, soft, leather sofa sat at the back edge of the rug. A matching ottoman big enough to nap on was in front of it. Large, matching, recliners flanked the sofa. Juliet had banked the fire before leaving. It was smoldering. She took a poker and rolled the banked logs over. Sparks flew up the chimney. She added some wood and soon there were flames. The logs were apple, cut from an old orchard down around Monroe by Lake Erie. She loved the apple and could afford to have it cut and transported. It sputtered and popped and had a wonderful odor. Juliet had made one concession to the architect. At the end of the room was a loft where she slept. A magnificent walnut spiral staircase led to it. A local craftsman had made it. There was an alcove with a four by six foot window from which she could see Jacker Point and the lake beyond. Occasionally she could see all the way to St. Ignace. She had her computer there and it was there that she became Della Queen and wrote her novels. She was working on one currently, entitled, "Winner Take All". There was a small bath and shower.

She invited him to sit in either of the large lounge chairs. He chose the one to the left of the davenport. She sat at the end nearest him,

"What do you drink?"

He just about said, *"Anything"*, but he had learned to think before blurting out the obvious,

"Whatever you're having will be fine."

"Well, I'm having some Chivas Regal. It's a cognac night."

"That's fine."

She walked to the right of the fireplace laid her hand on a piece of cherry and a liquor closet came swinging out of the wall. She dropped the lid, took out two enormous glasses and poured a healthy amount it each. She handed him one and bent over to clink glasses,

"Here's to the Lakers. I can't believe you took me to a basketball game."

"Two," he said.

"I was twice as dumb the second time. But really, it was fun. It was fun. Cold, but fun. But don't ask me again."

"Some day I'll show you a real sporting event and take you to an Ohio State football game."

"Oh, no! I hate football. That's all these people do up here after the first day it snows is watch football on TV. No thanks."

He didn't belabor the point. Instead he took a drink of the cognac. Smooth, and it warmed him inside. Juliet piled on two more logs. They popped and sparks flew against the screen. No words were spoken. It was too perfect for conversation. They drained their glasses and she poured more. Healthy amounts – this girl did not stint. He liked that. Most of the light came from the fire. The lanterns gave off only a mellow glow. Ira was warm from top to tip. The warmth from the fire first played upon his woolen socks. His feet, which had been icy, were now warm and tingled some. In fact a lot of his body tingled and it tingled more with each sip of the wonderful Chives Regal. She sipped hers – warmed her up, too.

"It's not the best, but it's dammed good," she said.

"Ummm" he said. He almost said, "Kind of like you," but as I said he was learning to think before speaking.

"On duty tomorrow? It's Sunday?" she asked in a voice that sounded as if she didn't want him to be.

"Yep. Six. Gonna' miss church. I relieve Slim.""

She knew he never attended church, but said nothing concerning it, "You can put the foot-rest up with that handle". At her end of the couch she was within touching distance. She wished he would.

He pulled the handle. The footrest came out and the back went back. He was as completely at ease as he had ever been. Ever. He shouldn't have done it, but he did. No, he did not touch her – he closed his eyes. In a matter of seconds a low rumble came from the chair. She smiled. She expected it. She rose, put three chunks of apple wood on the fire and a wool blanket over him. That would be the heat for the night. No furnace, she liked a cold bedroom. She climbed the spiral staircase, brushed her red hair one-hundred times, put on her only frilly night gown, lay down, pulled up a great, goose-down coverlet and wished he was beside her.

She shook him gently, "It's five-thirty" She wore a heavy robe over the frilly nightgown.

He jerked, "What the hell."

"The hell is you went to sleep on me." And handed him a cup of freshly made coffee. She'd gotten up early and was quiet, "I know you take it black."

"Thanks. My God. I'm sorry. What time is it?"

"You have nothing to be sorry over. You had a good nights sleep, next to a great fire." Which was now ashes. "It's five minutes later than when I woke you up."

"Well, I got to go. Everyone knows that nothing upsets me more than to have one of the guys come in late." He leaned forward, the back came up, the footrest went down.

He did not look well. He had a day's beard, he was out of uniform and his hair was what we used to call "Bus Hair".

Nevertheless, coffee cup in hand he walked to the door, found his coat and boots, said, "That's great cognac and one hell of a chair," and trudged off to the station. He got there just as Saint Anne's struck six.

"You look pretty rough," remarked Ed Dickerson, "Look like you slept standing up. Did you hear about the game lat night? We stalled and Teddy Freeman hit a jump shot at the buzzer."

"Yeah, I was there."

"You couldn't get in that bad of shape going to a basketball game."

"What can I say."

"Say nothing, it's your business."

"Right. Could you go to Darlene's and pick up my uniform?"

"It would be nice if the chief had on a uniform. Yeah, I'll get it."

"Thanks, I'll do the same for you sometime."

"I don't think so."

Ira shaved in the bathroom. It was a long day. Luckily nothing other than the usual happened.

Slim stopped in after church, "You still look like hell."

CHAPTER ELEVEN

That was the only game the Lakers won. They were one and twenty-one. By contrast, that was the Saints only loss. They finished nineteen and one and went deep into the state tournament before finally getting beat by Rogers City. The Ice Bridge lasted sixty-three days – second longest since records began. Neither Ira nor Juliet crossed it again that winter.

Ira saw little of Juliet. There's not much to do on the island when the winter is deep – except to wait for spring. Juliet did not invite Ira to her house. Horseback riding was out of the question – the snow was deeper than the horses were high. The sleigh races had all been run earlier. The island sat and waited. There was very little crime – not enough to write about – no drug use – a little marijuana.

Spring came grudgingly. It was early April before the ice melted enough to see open water. Regular ferry service started in mid-April. No one came to the island. The Grand opened and offered their Mother's Day weekend special which was from May seventh to May ninth that year. The special included accommodations with a full breakfast and dinner daily. There was a Friday evening welcome reception. Saturday featured a history lecture concerning the Grand and that evening there was another reception. On Mother's Day there was a wonderful buffet. Green fees were free on the Grand's Jewel Course but the course looked like hell and the greens were still frostbitten. The cost was *only* $650. Ira wondered where anyone got that kind of money, but that's who comes to the Grand – people with money. There were few takers since as indicated spring came very late that year. As soon as the Grand opened, however, Ira noticed a spike in the use of drugs. He never caught anyone in possession of them but he found plenty of seasonals high on them –

marijuana for certain and he knew the signs of heroin and crack. Every time he tried to find the source it was always the same, "Oh, I got it off of a fudgie. It was a one time hit."

The week after Mother's Day, Juliet dropped in at the station. She did stop and ask Janet if she "could see the Chief." It had warmed up some, but the wind from the north could still be bitter. She asked if he wanted to go sailing. Of course he did – and they did – more than once – several times. It was obvious she was training him for the race. He knew it, she knew it – everyone on the island knew it. She would not admit it, he certainly would not admit it – everyone else did admit it. "She's gettin' 'im ready for the race," said Forrest Reingold, owner of Forrest's Forest, the only flower shop on the island.

They sailed nearly every week on his day off. Acey and Deucey were always aboard. Ira didn't care for it but since he was not the captain he had no vote. It was obvious she was devoted to the dogs and they to her. Wherever she went they went also and crowded around her until she sent them off. At least they quit smelling his crotch after a while. *I guess they recognize me.* They always stopped for lunch. She always paid. Even suffered him a cigar at lunch over a last beer. It was a two beer limit for him, "Hey, you may have to drive," she said. He learned more than he wanted to. He learned what offshore and onshore winds were, that a lee-shore wind was dangerous as it could drive you on to land. To work yourself clear of a lee-shore you had to "claw" off. He learned she had Marconi sails, that the luff was the forward edge and the leech the aft edge. The foot of course was the lower edge and a bolt rope sewed into the edge of a sail strengthened it. He learned about battens and learned to insert them. He knew what a spinnaker was, although they did not use one. He learned that a jury mast was any spar rigged temporarily and that's where the term "jury rigged" came from. He was taught to reef a sail if the winds grew too strong and how to tie a reef point around the foot of the sail. He really wanted nothing to do with the race, but if she asked him again – well, he might consider it. Their love life was stymied; it got no further than it had the night he'd gone to sleep in her soft leather lounge chair. She kissed him after practice – and that's what it was – sailing practice. But they were more like pecks – not like that slow lingering kiss she'd given him that Friday night after they'd walked the ice bridge to St. Ignace to see the ball game.

The weather was much improved by the time the Lilac Festival came around. It started June eleventh and went through the thirtieth. Ira knew that in Columbus lilacs would have bloomed in mid-April. When the lilacs do bloom the whole island is enveloped in the most delicate fragrance and there is little in nature with perfume more delightful than a lilac. The festival has been held annually since the early fifties and some bushes on the island are over two-hundred years old.

It was glorious that week. The fudgies were back in number. Ira thought it was the best week he'd seen yet on the island. The girl who hosted lunch at the Island House was elected Lilac Queen. Her name was Caitlin Smart and it was her Ira had seen when he'd taken Clyde and Rosetta Stone there for a farewell dinner the previous summer and had lewd thoughts about. She was seventeen. Later in the week she won the 10 K run in her age division. Quite the girl – Ira thought. Then he recalled Rosetta earlier words. "You are familiar with San Quentin Quail." He was, and had other thoughts.

On July first, which was a Thursday that year, Juliet called Ira at the station,

"Got dinner plans tonight?"

Well, he never had dinner plans. It cost an arm and a leg to eat anywhere on the island and while some restaurant owners sometimes gave him a break, most did not, especially off season where every dollar seemed to count. Mostly he ate at Darlene's if she fixed him something or whatever he fixed in the microwave.

"Why?"

"Well, I've got two big rib-eyes over here. I should have just bought one. They are the best steak going. I work a mean grill and do potatoes, too. Just thought if you didn't have plans you might keep a lonely lady company."

Ira knew she wasn't lonely. He knew she loved her own company. All she needed was some wine, music, a fire in the winter and a good book and she was set for a month. She had a motive and it was not sex.

"I love rib-eyes. You know I don't get off 'til six. What time?"
"How about eight?"

"Well I'll be damned hungry by then. Okay – at eight."

Ed Dickerson came in to relieve him at six,

"Understand you're eating with the Steinbrenner's tonight."

Ira was astounded. She had called him not more than a couple of hours ago and here stood his deputy, who knew all about it,

"News travels fast on the island doesn't it?"

"Don't forget, I'm married – news travels fast among the women and then filters down to us men. Marge told me just as I was leaving. Said something about rib-eye steaks."

Ira rolled his eyes.

Ira knew good beer and bourbon but not much about wine. He bought the best bottle he could afford. He'd asked Martha at Doud's Market and she'd steered him towards a nice Merlot. "Good body and a nice bouquet."

Ira thought she'd just described Juliet.

He dressed up. Not a suit and tie, but dress pants, a long sleeved dress shirt – even though it was July when the sun went down it was cool. He shined his black shoes, wore calf-high black socks. No hat. He walked up. Smoked a cigar on the way. Threw it away before he got to her house. He was down to two-hundred sixteen and a lot more of it was muscle.

She had seen him coming and opened the door before his foot hit the first step,

"Aha, Pine Ridge a nice California Merlot from Doud's. I was wondering what I was going to serve with dinner. Now I know." Actually she had an expensive white Chilean wine she was going to serve but dinner had a purpose and the Chilean wine would not have served the purpose. "Here, let me have it. I'll chill it just a bit. Red wines need chilled very little."

She led him to the den, but not to the chair he'd fallen asleep in. She motioned him to sit on the wonderful leather couch. She stood,

"I've got a wine chilled. It's a white wine – not nearly so good as that Merlot. Best served before dinner. Care for a glass? I'm going to have one."

"Yeah, sure. I'm game. I don't know anything about wine, anyway."

She laughed a nervous laugh. Ira noticed it. It was not like her to be nervous. She was always so self assured,

"Okay, I'll get us one. I'll be right back."

Juliet uncorked her $169. bottle of white wine from the cellars of Santa Margarita and poured him a healthy glass – her, considerably less.

"Here we are. Put your feet up on the ottoman. It's only a fair wine, but I think you'll like it. Make yourself at home."

"Can I smoke a cigar?" He knew the answer. He was testing her. He wanted to see how far she'd go to get him to help crew the Little Sassy .

"Oh," she said, "You wouldn't be able to appreciate the flavor of the wine."

He smiled inside. She wasn't about to have that stinking cigar in her house. She'd man the Little Sassy by herself first. But he didn't mind. He was testing her – just to see how badly she needed him. Maybe he'd get lucky. He wasn't certain he would try that.

She sat beside him. They chatted – she about Lady Blue and the Little Sassy. He about police work and the rise of drug use on the island,

"I don't care so much about the liquor. Kids drink beer. But I sure as hell don't like what's goin' on out there with coke and horse. And you know what? You can't pin a damn thing on anyone. Never find any on them. They all claim they bought it off some fudgie – some fudgie who came over for a day or two. Don't buy that. There's someone on the island supplying it."

She showed concern, "Yes, people come here to retire and live the good life. Families come here to raise kids. It's a good place. There's no place on the island for hard drugs."

This went on for a half hour and she said, "Well, I know you said you'd be 'damn hungry' by eight so I assume you'll be starved my nine so I'll go do the steaks."

"Good, I'll come watch – if you don't mind."

"Sure."

She had the steaks laid out. Her kitchen was all stainless steel. She had a gas grill with a large hood. First she wrapped a couple of large Idaho potatoes in tin foil and laid them on the grill.

"I don't like potatoes wrapped in tin foil in a restaurant but that's about the only way you can do them on a grill."

She fussed with a salad in a large wooden bowl while the potatoes baked. Not a prissy salad – no raisins, cranberries, walnuts or curled carrots. She knew what she was playing at. If there is such a thing as a man's salad this was man's salad. A head of lettuce, mostly heart, was the basis. She took two juicy tomatoes, none of those hard island things – they had to come from Ohio or the like – cut them into eighths. Took a cucumber and cut some healthy slices – no thin things you could put over your eyes – sliced up some radishes, both white and red, added a half can of large black olives. Then sprinkled a healthy crumbling of blue cheese over the whole caboodle.

By that time the potatoes were half done. That's when she threw on the steaks,

"How do you like it?"

He looked at her,

"Medium-well."

"I suspected. You've probably not seen too many like me – I like it rare."

Indeed, she kind of shoved hers off to the side halfway through. She stuck a fork into the potatoes,

"A couple more minutes."

She let his steak grill for another two or three minutes and stuck the fork into the potatoes again,

"They're done and so's your steak. Hand me your plate." Her plates were square. That was the first time he'd seen that.

She speared his steak and placed it on his plate. Red juices seeped beneath it. She picked up the potato with a mittened hand and placed it on his plate. Did the same to hers.

"Help yourself to the salad. I've made a fresh vinegar and olive oil dressing," and she gave him a large wooden spoon and fork – not attached. He did.

"Is that okay"

Actually he was a thousand island man but at this stage, vinegar and oil looked just dandy.

He cut into his steak. Perfect. Just the way he liked it. A little juicy, kind of a pink but not rare – not red. And he was starving. It was a lot closer to nine than eight. She'd chilled the Merlot, just somewhat. He opened it and poured each a healthy amount. Actually he preferred the so called inferior Chilean white wine to his Merlot, but he said nothing.

"Sour cream for your potato?"

"No, thanks. I'm a butter man and he cut four slabs and laid two on each half. Then he ground some pepper on each half and shook more salt on his potato then she'd ever seen,

"You know, too much salt is not good for you."

"Sue me."

Her steak was dripping – red. He kind of looked away, but if that's the way she liked it. He should have offered something up about her red meat – but again held his tongue.

"I know it looks gross, but it's so tender. You really should try it sometime."

"I'll pass."

"Try a bite."

"I'll pass again."

It was a special meal, no doubts. Rib steaks have more fat than any steak and he was into fat that night. His was superb. The potato was genuine Idaho and one of their best. Actually he was a salad man and it was just as he would have made it himself – no, that's not true it was twice as good as if he'd made it himself. Hard, hard rolls – crusty with poppy seeds. They demolished the bottle of Merlot.

He didn't know about it but she brought out a peach cobbler straight from the oven. Oh, god. His favorite. She couldn't have known. A pure guess.

"The peaches are from my tree. Picked them today."

It was still very warm and did not need any microwaving. She brought out a pint of half and half. She could have asked him anything at that point and he would have acquiesced.

He was stuffed. Longed for a cigar.

"Can I help with the dishes?"

"Yes, you may, but first let's take a walk. I know you're just itching to light up one of those terrible cigars. I'll walk up-wind."

Even in July the evenings could be cool and though Juliet wore long sleeves she shivered some. Ira lit his cigar and she did walk up-wind – there's always a breeze on the island. He took her hand and they walked downtown. It was the height of the tourist season and some shops were still open, but it was pushing ten.

"Let's stop at the station and see how things are."

Officer Upland was on duty. It was quiet, very little going on. It wasn't the weekend. He'd go out about midnight and help the drunks – break up any fights.

It was a lot steeper going back than coming. He was nearly done with his cigar and thought she'd suffered enough so he threw it away. *Littered,* he thought. He'd pick it up on the way back.

Back inside and back on the wonderful leather couch she asked him if he'd like another glass of Chilean wine. He would.

They small talked a while and then she hit him with it. He knew she would,

"Well, what do you think about it?" she asked, point blank.

"About what?" he countered.

"You know what I'm referring to," again pointedly.

"Sex? Oh, yeah. I'm for that. When do we start?" He thought, *If she's going to make me squirm, I'm going to make her squirm, too.*

It surprised her – embarrassed her. Her pale face reddened. Almost matched her hair. She realized she'd gone at it all wrong. She was flustered. She could only mutter – weakly – hardly audible,

"That will be the day."

"What? Did you say – today?"

"I said that will be the goddam day," with authority.

"Look, Juliet, if you want me to help you sail the Little Sassy in this race which I know nothing about nor do I know nothing about sailing – why don't you just ask me."

Most of the time she was so self assured, now the façade was slipping,

"Well, will you?"

"Let me ask you a question. Why is this race so dammed important to you? It means nothing to me. Why would I get involved in something I care nothing about?"

"I'll tell you why. I've lived on this island all my life. I learned to sail before I could ride a bike. My grandfather and I sailed together from the time I could walk. My grandfather entered this race seventeen straight times. I was with him the last seven. He was runner-up, once. I told him I'd win that damned trophy and I intend to do it."

"Then you should get you a hand who knows what the hell he's doing. I don't know much about sailing, but isn't a crew of two a little shy on personnel in this type of race."

"No. You know all the lines and how to handle them. You're strong enough to do the work and the boom has not hit you – yet. I don't trust anyone else on this island. In addition, the more people there are, the more chances there are for screw-ups. A two man crew is just right."

"Now, is not this race a two or three day thing and when you're sleeping who's gonna' run the boat?"

"You."

"But I don't know a damn thing about guiding a boat."

"You don't guide them, you steer them or more properly you pilot them."

"Well, I cannot do either."

"You don't have to; they steer themselves – by computers. Besides, I'm not going to sleep eight hours. I'll lie down for a half hour or so and that will be it. I've done this a dozen times."

"Well, why don't you go and get some of those people who have sailed with you before?"

"There were no other people; I do it myself – that's why I've never won."

"You mean you just let the boat sail itself?"

"That's right."

"Aren't you afraid you'll hit another boat or a rock or something?"

"Let me tell you, those boats are spread out and you just put it on automatic pilot and it holds the course. There are no rocks on the course."

"When is this damned race?"

"July seventeenth."

"Well, I didn't start my job until August. I have no vacation days."

"Let me worry about that."

He'd already made up his mind to do it. He didn't want her to beg – of course she never would. He liked this girl – she was independent, yet vulnerable. You can be both. He didn't want to do it, as he really thought he did not know enough about sailing to be of much help. But what the hell, at least he would be company and he could do some of the physical work Juliet would have trouble doing. Besides three days on a boat with Juliet could be fun.

"Okay, I'll do it, but you don't know what you're getting yourself in for."

"Oh, that's wonderful," she was genuinely excited, "You'll do just fine. Let's have another glass of that white wine."

"You mean that inferior wine."

She grinned, "Yours was a good wine."

CHAPTER TWELVE

From that day they sailed every day Ira was not on duty. He improved each day. They were becoming a team. Katy McCormack arranged an early week of vacation for Ira,

"Gonna be a long time before your next one."

"Yeah, and this is just the way I wanted to spend my vacation."

"She needs someone like you."

"Well, I can tell you I'm not doing it for me."

Clyde and Rosetta Stone came to the island for their two week holiday. They stayed at the Mohawk. Contrary to Rosetta's hopes and, perhaps, Clyde's, he was elected mayor of Kankakee for another two year term. Ira visited as much as possible. Sat out on the verandah and drank Rosetta's gin and tonics. She had a pitcher of them made up and kept filling his glass. Every morning he had a headache. He smoked his cigars and they did not mind – at least they said nothing. Took them to dinner a couple of times. Once with Juliet along. Julie just adored Rosetta and the feeling was more than mutual. Once he took them to the Island House where Miss Lilac was still hostess. Ira tried not to salivate over her. Rosetta reminded him,

"Eighteen's the legal age and you're what, forty-six? She's seventeen. That's only thirty years difference. I'm certain you impress her. My suggestion is you have the same thoughts about that nice Juliet Steinbrenner."

The July 4th celebration was civil. The fireworks display at the old fort was spectacular. Every year there was speculation whether or not there would be enough money for fireworks. It was always a near thing. The display was one of the best in the Midwest and was costly. But Mayor Katy and the Chamber of Commerce people thought it necessary for the community to put on such a display to satisfy the tourists and to attract more next year. The Grand Hotel gave a bushel of money and so did many of the other merchants and a lot of the locals, too. They knew the island depended on tourists.

There were the usual drunks, both tourists and seasonal workers. One young man from the Mohawk threw up on him. Ira gave Jack Walsh shit over it, "Damn, if I'da known that I'da given him to you, first." Several, more than he wanted to see, were high on drugs. *Damn, this drug thing is getting out of hand. As soon as this race is over I'm going to get to the bottom of it.*

After the Fourth of July every day Ira had off he was on the Little Sassy. He was becoming more and more at ease on the boat. He was beginning to, as they say in nautical terms, "learn the ropes."

On July thirteenth they left for Chicago. They had a heated argument before they even got under weigh. When Ira arrived carrying his duffel bag the first thing he heard was the barking of dogs. There, hanging paws over the railing and barking like mad, were Acey and Deucey. That brought Juliet to the rail. He yelled from the dock,

"You're not taking those dogs with you, are you?"

"Sure am!"

"But all they're gonna' to do is run all over and crap and bark and who's going to take care of them?"

"They've been with me on every race."

"They'll bark all the time. Jesus. How many other rigs will have dogs on them?"

"I don't know but I know one that will."

He'd lost. He knew it. It was her damned boat, but had he known about the dogs he wasn't certain he'd have gone. *He'd end up feeding and taking care of them.* He just knew it.

"For Christ's sake, Juliet. Dogs in a damned race."

The wind was brisk from the north and blew them into Chicago in forty-seven hours. The weather forecast for the race was for fair weather with gusty winds from the north. Winds up to twenty-five knots. They'd have to fight them on the return trip. Predicting weather is not an exact science they were to learn later.

Juliet kept her word; she slept very little and anytime Ira was at the helm she kept a close watch. They did not use the automatic pilot, she wanted him to get used to steering by compass. Juliet also took care of the dogs.

After they docked, they left their racing gear on the boat and took only the bare necessities with them. Although for Juliet the "bare necessities" were two good sized travel bags. She called on her cell phone and had a white Lincoln limo waiting. It took them to the Drake on Walton Street, a venerable Chicago landmark that had been there since the twenties. Grandfather Charlie had stayed there before every race including the last seven when Juliet had been his crew. It was old but fashionable. As soon as they arrived some young man in uniform took the dogs. They whimpered at first but went along after Juliet fussed over them somewhat.

Any big name who came to Chicago stayed at the Drake. Juliet and Ira were only to be there two nights. Juliet reserved two small adjoining suites that overlooked Lake Michigan. Each had a bedroom, sitting area and balcony. The Chicago Yacht Club was to hold a "Warning Gun" reception hosted by the sponsor Veuve Clicquot, maker of some of the world's best Champagne. Juliet eschewed the celebration, "I want to keep my mind on the race."

They ate dinner in the Coqd'or Room. Marilyn Monroe and Joe DiMaggio had eaten in the same room and had carved their initials on the bar. Ira had two orders of escargot, a wonderful barley soup, king sized prime rib – rubbed with sea salt, potatoes augratin and white asparagus. No salad. *By God, if I have to do this I'm gonna' get something out of it.*

She ordered the wine – Pine Ridge Merlot at sixty-two dollars a bottle.

Juliet ate salad. He couldn't tell what kind – he could see an abundance of shrimp. She drank several glasses of wine – more than he and they finished the bottle.

They took the elevator to their suites,

"Don't get any ideas."

He hadn't any.

"I'm going to bed early. I'm going to get my rest. Just like that Ohio State football team of yours, I'm in training and the only thing on my mind is that cup. I aim to win it."

Ira felt no pressure. All he had to do was do what she said. He thought he knew enough about the Little Sassy to do what she wanted.

At her door she said,

"Figure out what you want for breakfast and put it on the door outside. Put the time on it and they'll bring it. I plan to sleep in so if you get up early – well, Chicago is a big town – go see some of it."

He was bushed. He filled out the card for seven o'clock – hot oats with brown sugar, double order of wheat toast, a whole lot of black coffee and pineapple juice.

He watched a little of the Cubs game. It wasn't the same since Harry Carey had died, but Steve Stone was tolerable. He liked the Cubs second to the Indians – who were almost as pitiful. The combined years since either had won a world series added up to one-hundred sixty. Both were pathetic – though Cleveland *had* been in the World Series in nineteen ninety-four and again in nineteen ninety-seven – lost them both.

Ira was showered and dressed when the room service brought breakfast. He was hungry and ate quickly. A bell hop brought in a copy of the Chicago Tribune. The Cubs had lost, the Indians had won. In the art section he read about an exhibition of Van Goughs at the Chicago Museum of Fine Art. Ira did not know art but he knew Van Goughs and loved them all. He finished the paper and pot of coffee at the same time. He was not used to being idle and his part in the race was one of "do what I tell you to do", so he was not concerned. He took a cab to the museum. They had a dazzling display of Van Goughs including *Sower with Setting Sun, The Arlesienne, Madame Ginoux with Books, La Crau with Peach Blossoms in Bloom, Two Poplars, Field with Poppies* and Ira's favorite, *The Starry Night*.

He had lunch in the museum coffee shop – a sandwich and another pot of coffee. He bought a book of Van Gough's paintings by Hans Bronkhorst and spent a good part of the afternoon looking it over. More coffee. He made up his mind if he could ever afford it he'd go to Holland and visit the Rijksmuseum in Amsterdam. A friend of his had been there and told him it was fantastic.

It was pushing five when he arrived back at the Drake. It was the fist time he'd spent all day in any museum – ever. He knocked on Juliet's door. She was wearing one of the Drake's five-pound terrycloth robes and did not offer to let him in,

"You been in that all day?"

"That race's a bitch. I need all the rest I can get. I suggest you get a good night's sleep. The cannon goes off tomorrow morning at eleven-thirty – our section is at thirteen-thirty – that's one-thirty to you"

Ira rolled his eyes. *I'm not stupid* – instead he said,

"Are you going to have dinner?"

"Room service."

"Why don't we have room service in my room?"

"That's the last place, Buster, where I will be eating tonight. I'm eating alone – here."

Knowing she had just accused him of trying to get her into bed the night before the big race she was smart enough to reach up and give him a brush of a kiss on the lips,

"Let's see what happens after we win the race," Juliet said – softly.

Many words and thoughts went through Ira's mind, but he said,

"Okay, see you in the morning."

"We'll leave the hotel at six."

Ira ate in the Cape Cod room – shrimp cocktail, filet mignon – medium well. A baked potato – no aluminum foil, broccoli – he loved it. Two beers with dinner and another while he smoked the blackest cigar you have ever seen. Bought it there at the hotel. Black as a fan belt.

It was a fact that there would be a great deal going on at the Club on Friday. Many participants and crews were on the docks preparing their boats. Then there was the pre-race party Friday evening to celebrate the start of the race on Saturday,

"I've been to a dozen of those things. All they do is distract you and some of the party boys get so drunk they can barely sail the next day. They're not in it to win anyway; they're in it to socialize. I'm in it to win."

CHAPTER THIRTEEN

Juliet was pounding on his door at five-thirty. He figured she would be early and he was ready. He'd had room service coffee at five. She paid the bill and collected the dogs. They were all over her and smelled his crotch again – *damn dogs, you'd think by now they'd know me.* The same limo took them to the Little Sassy. It was a brilliant day – the north wind still blowing strong. It had not let up since their arrival. As soon as they boarded Juliet called the National Weather Service for the weather: *clear in the morning, partly cloudy in the afternoon, winds from the northwest at ten to fifteen knots, seas – four to six feet.* Ira knew enough about sailing to know that a knot-per-hour-wind was faster than a mile-per-hour-wind. Juliet wrinkled her brow and said,

"Stiff wind. Lots of tacking."

They spent hours going over the boat, checking everything. Juliet left nothing to chance. Every detail was attended to. They changed the sails four times, just for practice and to inspect each sail. The dogs were by her side each step of the way until she shooed them off.

The race begins at the mouth of the Chicago River, goes north the entire length of Lake Michigan, barely gets into Lake Huron and finishes in the Round Island Channel off Mackinac. Oddly enough the course is exactly three-hundred thirty-three miles long and is marked with buoys. The race is sponsored by the Chicago Yacht Club and three-hundred seven boats were ready to start when the Commodore of the Club set off the cannon.

It's not a scramble. The first section, the Doublehanded, starts at eleven-thirty. Sections follow every ten minutes. It's not a race against fellow boaters. It's a race against time. The Little Sassy did not exactly spring forth from her berth. With winds from the northwest she was being blown away from the course. Ira did as he was ordered and Juliet kept the boat north as best she could, but they were being constantly blown east. They were making about three knots. By marine time it was 20:30 before they took time to eat. They ate cold food, mainly sandwiches fixed by the Drake.

It stays light well past nine o'clock at that latitude and time of the year. It was cool, not cold. They both were in windbreakers. True to her word Juliet sailed the Little Sassy through the night, napping only occasionally and engaged the automatic pilot when Ira took the helm. The wind picked up through the night to a steady fifteen knots – gusting to twenty. Long before dawn Ira could tell it was cloudy. The day was sullen; the winds grew stronger. The clouds were low and scudding, occasionally settling on the water - fog – not thick and treacherous but annoying. There was no sign of the sun which had been so brilliant the day before. They ate a cold breakfast – fruit and cereal. The cereal almost impossible to eat as the boat was moving up and down and side to side. Juliet did brew a pot of coffee which was surprisingly good. Ira needed it very much. They had at least thirty hours to go.

Juliet checked the weather and was not happy: higher winds – twenty to twenty-five knots, more clouds, a falling barometer and rain. They could see other boats – none close. The "Bluebell" was off the portside bow a half mile or so. Ira, ignorant of most boat racing knowledge, knew it was windy, cloudy and cool enough to break out his hooded sweatshirt. They were off Ludington. As the day wore on, the conditions grew worse. The day was sullen, the wind becoming stronger by the hour, clouds low and scudding, occasionally settling on the water – fog. Shortly after noon it started to rain. It did not start as a sprinkle and lead into a rain. It started as a downpour and stayed that way – drenching. Ira was surprised at how cold it was, *Damn, it's damned near August.* But Ira was thinking of August in Columbus. The water temperature was perhaps fifty-five degrees. Juliet broke out the yellow rain-slickers and they donned them gladly. More wind. The rain never abated. Sullen – miserable weather. Somehow Juliet was able to fix hot soup in the late afternoon. More hot coffee, too. It raised their spirits. There was no danger, just misery.

"Is it like this every race?"

She had to laugh, "This is my fifteenth and the second time it's rained – so the answer is, 'No'".

The seas were higher, six to eight feet. Ira was destined to find out if he did, indeed, suffer from seasickness. So far so good.

The bad weather continued: a hard rain, strong winds, high seas. It did not grow dark at nine that night. By eighteen-hundred it was dark. They navigated by compass and radar. They had a cold supper – Ira could not tell you what it was. He's forgotten. Too many other things happened that night. Juliet never left the helm. The wind had picked up considerably. The National Weather Service was reporting gusts of thirty knots. She put the dogs in the cabin.

The boat was flying even with the high seas, but she was flying east – right onto the state of Michigan which was a lot harder than the water they were on. Juliet fought to keep the Little Sassy on course. Ira stayed with her hunched under a little fly of nylon which leaked like a sieve.

Bad things on boats many times happen at night. It was at night when the Titanic struck the iceberg. Each passing hour brought higher winds, more rain and heavier seas. The Little Sassy wallowed from one trough to the next. She bobbed like a cork on a boy's fishing line. It was too dark to see anything but water and that was probably a good thing for they would not have liked the size of the waves the Little Sassy was fighting. Once when they crested high on a wave they saw the mast light of another vessel. They could not tell if it was coming, going, near or far. By midnight they were completely drenched through their neoprene slickers. They were chilled, hungry, miserable and pissed off – at least Ira was and he thought Juliet was, too. She said nothing though, nor did he. He'd learned to keep is mouth shut in trying times. He knew she was going to need him and they were going to need each other. The dogs whimpered and at times, wailed.

Afterward Juliet admitted she should have known better. She should have reefed the mainsail. She didn't and a sudden gust hit and ripped it from head to foot.

"Dowse the mains'il and unfurl and raise the mizzen sail," she ordered. He did.

The mizzen sail drew a full gust of wind and stared to chatter.

"Shorten the mizzen and tie it off." He did.

Together they replaced the mainsail, dowsed the mizzen but left it unfurled. They made sail with the mainsail – another error. The wind drew in the mainsail so hard it laid the boat over.

"Shorten the mains'l and reef it."

He did and the Little Sassy stabilized.

Ira could see she was wearing out. At one bell he took the helm – had no idea what he was doing – just knew that he was stronger than she. She stood behind him. The wind tore through her slicker and whipped her hair into a red fury – so hard it stung her face. By now the winds were gale force. The National Weather Service had issued warnings and urged all boats to get to port. That would have been nice – but impossible. He didn't know where they were and he was not certain she did. To cut the tension he yelled over the wind,

"Are we having fun, yet?"

"I'm sorry I got you into this. I doubt there's been this kind of weather in the history of this race. We need to put our life jackets on – now."

She went to the cabin and came back with two,

"Put it over your slicker."

"Well, you take the wheel." And he got into his preserver. It gave him no sense of security.

He started to take stock. He was not a strong swimmer. That damned water was cold as hell. He'd last a few hours at most. If the boat went down in the middle of the night he doubted he'd make it until dawn – maybe. He didn't know about Juliet and was not going to ask. She could volunteer.

"The dogs are scared," she said.

"Me, too," that was all he could say.

He kept at the helm, she squatting down trying to give him the course. It didn't matter, all he was trying to do was to keep it afloat. He couldn't see the waves. He only knew the direction they were sailing and which way the waves were running and tried to steer into them rather than be broadsided by them. As it was, water was coming over the bow and he could hear the bilge pumps working hard to clear it out.

Ira was not certain there would be a morning and was not certain he'd live to see it. The dark continued. During the summer the sun rises at five but it was eight bells before it got light enough to see the bow. He could see the waves and they numbed him. What he saw were four sides of water. The Little Sassy would climb up top of a huge comber and then the bottom would drop out and they slammed into the trough. The whole boat shuddered. *She can't take much more of this. There are three hundred and six other boat out there and we can't see a damned one.*

The National Weather Service again warned all boats to get to port. The winds were forecast at fifty knots, seas at twenty feet, the barometer was at 28.95 and falling. Not since the sinking of the Edmund Fitzgerald on Lake Superior had the barometer been that low and the wind that strong.

Ira had been at the helm for seven hours. Every fabric strained for relief. He had so much adrenalin pumping he had not thought once of going to the bathroom. All bodily functions had shut down. Juliet could have been lying there naked and all he would have wanted to know was – what course do I steer?

It didn't seem possible but the winds grew stronger and the seas – well, they looked like something out of The Poseidon Adventure or the Perfect Storm. The rain was blowing with such fury it cut anything that was exposed. Then they realized it was not rain but sleet and it pelted any exposed area mercilessly.

There had been a few flashes of lightning – they seemed far away – not near enough to worry over. Ira wondered – *it's too damned cold to have lightning.* He was dead wrong. Out of the caliginous came a thunderous boom. A bolt of lightning irradiated the whole of the Little Sassy. It was so bright it stunned them. It was several seconds before they could see. What they saw was Charlie Steinbrenner's wonderful work of art – his twenty foot oaken mast cleaved in two. Not having a knot in it the mast had split into two identical halves. There was not a quarter inch difference. One half fell on the starboard beam the other on the port. For an instant the Little Sassy took on the outline of a shrimp boat.

The heel of the mast was stepped in the keel. The mast wedges and mast partners were ripped off like toothpicks. How the mast remained in the mast hole at all was a tribute to Grandfather Charlie and his design. That did not last long. The boat pitched and yawed at the same instant and both halves joined Lake Michigan. The Little Sassy was demasted. At least in principal – the mizzen mast remained.

"Jesus Christ!" was all Ira could say. Now, Ira was one step to the right of atheism. He wasn't about to shout out loud there was no God, but he was convinced that Jesus Christ was not the only way to get there. If so, what was God going to do with the other three-fourths of the people of the world who were not Christians. But at the moment he was as close to a believer as he had been since his teens.

"Oh, goddamnit," cried Juliet, "look at Grandfather's mast."

Ira was staring at the great hole in the deck where the mast had been. He didn't see the wave until it was upon them. What he saw almost made him puke. It was the largest natural thing he'd ever seen. The Little Sassy rode her to the top and when the bottom fell out and they crashed he knew right away she was badly wounded. The helm spun around and the rudder went to the bottom of Lake Michigan. The boat went where it was taken.

"Get a life line on," Juliet said and with complete authority, "I'll let the dogs out and put a vest on them." She was shaking but her voice was strong. She was the captain and was giving orders. They had practiced a life line drill – once – and when you think about life lines you tend to remember. That's the thing that might save your life.

Juliet had just got her line secured and was trying to put a vest on Deucey when Ira looked out. What was coming at them made the last wave look like a piker. Ira knew the boat would not survive this one.

Ira never liked roller coasters. They didn't make him ill – they just scared the hell out of him. The coming wave was like the roller coaster at Coney Island. the Little Sassy made her last climb. The bottom of Ira's stomach fell out at the same time the bottom did of the Little Sassy. As it descended it stretched her from bow to stern so that Juliet's life line snapped like a rubber band. When they bottomed out Juliet went over the side in a flash. The dogs were thrown several feet into the air – Deucey was knocked unconscious. Acey stunned and whimpering. Ira, hanging on to the helm when she bottomed out lost his front teeth when his mouth hit the king spoke.

He spat out pieces of teeth. Both lips were split and blood ran down his slicker – the rain washing it away as fast as he bled.

Juliet was gone in an instant. Ira ran to the rail. He could just make out her yellow slicker and could see it was dragging her down. She was screaming frantically, "Throw the preserver! Throw the preserver!"He grabbed it. He threw it out, but Juliet could not get to it. He brought it in and threw it again. It wasn't even close. She was falling further and further behind the boat. He brought it in and tried it again. No go. Acey was going crazy, running back and forth, jumping the rail barking like a banshee. Ira did the only thing he could think of. He tied the line around Acey's neck and screamed above the howling wind,

"Go get her boy. For the love of God, go get her." And Ira threw him in.

Now, Acey was a powerful dog, but he was no Labrador, he was no swimmer. Great Danes were bred in Germany to hunt boars – not to retrieve ducks. Acey had no idea where to go or what to do and started swimming back to the boat. Ira pointed in Julie's direction– he could barely see the yellow slicker,

"That way boy," he shouted but his words had no effect.

Juliet was screaming as loud as she could, but the wind was howling so loudly she couldn't be heard. She couldn't be heard by human ears, that is. The Great Dane with its large ears can hear thing humans cannot and Acey caught the sound of Juliet's voice. He swam towards her. Juliet kept screaming. Dogs cannot think – they know not, but such was the devotion of Acey to Juliet he swam in her direction – not knowing he may never return. Most of the time it was impossible for Ira to see Juliet from the rail – he knew the dog could not. Acey just followed the sound of Juliet's screaming.

All Ira could see was a small dot of yellow and occasionally a smaller dot of brindle but Acey was gaining ground. The wind was shrieking, the rain was unabated – more sleet than rain – the dog threshed – Juliet screamed – the line was running out. Juliet could not move, she was exhausted and suffering from hypothermia. It all depended on Acey and the length of the line. Acey was spent; he made little headway. Like the great athlete he was he'd spent it – he had nothing left.

Juliet pleaded, "Acey! Here Acey! Here boy! Here! Over here!". The line ran out – Acey stopped. There was no more. How close? Thirty, maybe forty feet. Juliet saw Acey go under. No one ever said Juliet was not a fighter. She may have been rich, but she kept in top shape. She made one last desperate effort. She put her head under water and thrashed toward Acey. The distance narrowed, an agonized bit – twenty feet now. Again Acey went under – more threshing – ten feet. Acey went under taking the line with him. With his last dreadful effort he fought his way to the top. She was there. She grabbed him and the line at the same time.

"I've got it," she screamed.

Ira began pulling – the line was long – the load unbearable. The line was rough – he had no gloves. His hands were freezing. His mouth was bleeding – he spit out more slivers of enamel. It took all his effort to pull them a few feet. He was never going to make it – he knew it. He was never going to pull them both in.

"Let go that damn dog."

She didn't.

"For Christ's sake, let go that dog. I can't pull both of you. I can't do it."

"I can't."

"What do you mean – you can't?" he bellowed

"I mean I can't do it. I won't."

"Let loose that fuckin' dog. Or you're both gonna' drown."

"You watch your mouth, buddy. I won't! Now pull on this son-of-a-bitchin' line!"

She was so stubborn! Ira got pissed off so much he found strength from somewhere – a good Baptist would say from The Lord – but Ira did not believe in that. He got strength from those little glands that set on top of your kidneys. They can help you do superhuman feats. And little by little he began to win the battle. It took twenty minutes and it seemed twenty hours. When they got close enough to get them aboard he took the dog first.

"I'm saving this fuckin' mutt before I do you." And he grabbed the line around Acey's neck and hauled him aboard – nearly choking him to death in the process. Acey collapsed in a puddle of icy water – too spent even to shake himself.

"I said watch your language" and he had to laugh and I mean laugh as he grabbed her. It was an hysterical laugh. She weighed a ton – everything she wore held water. He had no strength left. His mouth once numb was killing him. In his effort he swallowed blood and parts of teeth. He just could not get her over the freeboard. He was numb from the cold and he could not think. His mind and body went into automatic. Later, he did not recall doing it but he tied the rope under Juliet's armpits and, placing both feet at the base of the gunnels, drug her aboard like a skewered whale. He tumbled backward and lost consciousness. Juliet passed out when she hit the deck.

Ira was unaware how long he was out but when he woke to the sound of howling wind the Little Sassy was filling with water. They still had power and he could hear the pumps straining to take out the water that was flooding in at an alarming rate. Ira struggled to his knees and crawled to the prostrate form of Juliet. Acey had not moved.

The boat was on its own and bobbing up and down like a Champaign cork in a bathtub. It went were it went. Ira struggled to pick up Juliet . She was dead weight. He carried her down to the cabin. It was wet, with the mast gone and water coming in. He stripped her and found three things: her breasts were larger than he thought, they had no freckles on them and her pubic hair was red and wild just like the hair on her head. He found an old wool army blanket that only her Grandfather Charlie could have put aboard. But it was dry and he wrapped her in it and laid her on a berth. Seconds later he was on the ships radio issuing a May Day. Much of the skin on both his palms was gone. He was dripping blood all over the radio. He took off his socks and wrapped them around his hands. He went directly to the Coast Guard frequency.

"May Day! May Day! This is the Little Sassy. We're taking on water, our rudder is gone. It's only a matter of time before we sink. I don't think we have time for a boat to get here. Send a chopper. I have no idea where we are, the skipper is unconscious, but I'd say we're somewhere between the Manitou Islands and the coast. May Day! May Day! Over."

"Little Sassy. This is the Coast Guard Cutter, Franklin. Hear you loud and clear. We have several boats in trouble. Break your life rafts out and get them ready. Stay on board as long as possible. But get into the rafts before she goes down or she'll take you with her. We'll be there ASAP. Over."

All of Ira's police and PI training came into play. He did not panic – he had never panicked. Juliet was still out, so was Acey. Deucey was stirring and whimpering. He went to the stern and grabbed the two rubber life rafts. The wind tore at him. When he activated the CO2 canisters on the first raft it inflated so quickly it nearly knocked him down. He stayed back from the second one. He tied them both fast to some davits and then started rounding up the passengers – people first.

He wanted to dress Juliet, but she was still unconscious and he couldn't take the time. He wrapped the blanket tightly around her, took off his belt and drew it up tight around her midsection. He carried her up to the deck, the boat heaving , and laid her in one of the rafts. Acey was still out and he carried him to the other – he weighed as much as Juliet. Deucey was trying to stand and wobbling all over the deck. He picked her up and did the same.

"Stay," he ordered. Deucey wasn't going anywhere.

He heard the pumps shut down, the power was gone. The boat was tossed to and fro. Ira dragged the raft with the dogs to the stern. The Little Sassy was heaving so that trying to get the raft into the water seemed an impossible task. When he grabbed it at both ends the dogs slid to the middle and as gingerly as possible he lowered it into the water and tied it off. The second raft held precious cargo. He tied a line to each end of the raft and using them as davits lowered the raft into the boiling water. Then he jumped in.

The water instantly numbed him. He was exhausted – not much adrenalin flowing now. Using all his strength, Ira pulled himself over the side and tumbled into the raft – too exhausted to move. He lay at the bottom, halfway on Juliet, for several minutes before he could gather the strength to move. When he was finally able to sit up he tied the raft with the dogs in it to their raft, untied it from the Little Sassy and shoved off. Very quickly the distance between the boat and rafts lengthened but not before he saw the bow of the Little Sassy slip beneath the cruel waters of Lake Michigan. Grandfather Charlie

Steinbrenner's wonderful creation joined hundreds of more vessels at the bottom.

The dogs wailed like the frightened creatures they were. None of their noises resembled a bark. Their noises reminded Ira of an old Sherlock Holmes movie he'd seen – The Hounds of Baskerville. The storm rather than abating grew in intensity. The rafts rode to the top of one wave, then another. The rain pelted them mercilessly. The blanket he'd fashioned around Juliet was soaked. Her henna colored hair was stringy and fell half across her face. As in Procul Harem's song her skin was a "whiter shade of pale." There were several inches of water in both rafts. Ira bailed with his hands but there was no one to help in the raft with the dogs. Ira wasn't going to try to help them – if they made it fine, if not, well, Acey would always be a hero.

Ira was numbed by the cold. He wanted to call it a day – a life. He wanted to give in. He wanted to close his eyes and drift into eternity – *"Out of the night that covers me, black as the pit from pole to pole – I thank whatever gods may be for my unconquerable soul"*, kept going through his mind. *"In the fell clutch of circumstance I have not wept nor cried aloud, under the bludgeonings of chance my head is bloody but unbowed. Beyond this place of wrath and tears looms but the horror of the shade and yet the passing of the years finds and shall find me unafraid,"* was all he could think of. He was unafraid – but he feared for Juliet's sake and he fought the cold with the will of his long ago Dempsey relative – the one he'd heard stories about over and over in boyhood – the Manassa Mauler. Juliet moaned.

He shook her shoulders – she moaned. He'd dreamed of making her moan but not in this fashion. Strange how that thought entered his mind. He shook her harder. She flickered. Then he slapped her sharp on one cheek.

"Wha—Wha—What – goddam it. What! What!"

"Wake up! Wake up!"

She sat bolt upright – kind of like you see a body do in a scary movie,

"Where's the Sassy! What the fuck did you do with the Sassy!"

"She's gone."

"Oh, Christ," and the tears rolled and turned to sobs,

"Not my Sassy. Not my beautiful Sassy. What will Grandpa think of me! Oh God!"

"She's gone and we may not be far behind."

"My dogs! My dogs!"

"They're in the raft tied behind us. Acey saved your life."

"I know. He loves me."

"I love you."

"I know."

No one is certain how long they were in the raft – both were unconscious when the Coast Guard helicopter spotted two small yellow dots in the vast expanse of Lake Michigan. Ira had been somewhat correct when he said they were near the Manitou's – but they were west of the islands. The helicopter had spent precious hours searching for them on the east side. It had not been a fruitless search for they had picked up survivors from four other boats that had gone down. They took Juliet first, her limp body strapped to her rescuer, and put aboard the chopper. Ira was next – the dogs last. Deucey didn't make it. It was thought that when she was slammed against the deck at the fall of the great wave she was injured internally and bled to death while she was in the raft. Acey was still breathing.

Ira and Juliet were taken to the hospital in Traverse City, a small but highly specialized hospital. They were put in the same room – both suffering gravely from hypothermia. Doctors were uncertain if they would live. Acey went to the best veterinary hospital in town where a very skilled vet by the name of Dr. Bogenrife kept him alive.

Their youth and condition pulled them through. Ira was thankful about the thirty pounds he'd lost over the year by riding his cop-bike and otherwise walking. Juliet was despondent over losing the Little Sassy, but after she learned that fourteen other boats had sunk and another thirty-two were so badly damaged they had to be towed by the Coast Guard she realized they had done their best. The race was never finished – the first time since it was inaugurated in 1908. No winner was declared. No one had perished, but there were others like Ira and Juliet who were lucky to have survived. It was several days before Juliet was informed of the death of Deucey. She cried and blamed herself for bringing her. It was then Ira reminded her that if she hadn't taken the dogs she wouldn't be alive,

"I'll get me another one – and another boat too – just like the Sassy. I'm going to have another boat – just like the Sassy."

Ira thought both were good ideas.

"What was the last thing you said to me before I conked out?" This was Juliet.

"I forget."

"I knew you would."

"I know where you don't have any freckles."

"And I know where you don't have any brains."

It was several more days before they were released. Clive and Rosetta Stone were there from the first day,

"People are bitchin' and gripin' 'cause I ain't at my desk. I told them to go piss up a rope."

Rosetta shopped for clothing for Juliet. Ira wore what he had on. The Stones drove them back to Mackinac – all they possessed was what they had on their back – and Acey.

Acey wouldn't let Juliet out of his sight and insisted on being beside her the entire trip.

CHAPTER FOURTEEN

The pair, along with Acey, were treated as heroes. Acey was given a medal and a citation by the fire chief. Juliet framed the citation and hung it over the mantel along with the pictures of Mother, Father and Grandfather. Juliet placed the medal around Acey's neck where it hung proudly until Acey chased a chipmunk and caught the medal on something and was nearly strangled. After that she made a place for it on the mantle.

Ira returned to work after two days back. He owed the island time for being gone longer than he had been authorized. Katy McCormack said she'd take it out of next year's vacation time. Juliet climbed her spiral staircase and slept for two days – Acey at the foot of her bed. Ira saw a dentist in St. Ignace who made him a great partial for his missing front teeth. As I said the pair was treated as heroes for a short time – right up until the night Teddy Freeman died from overdosing on a cocaine cocktail.

The headline on the Mackinac Island Town Crier read:

LOCAL STAR ATHLETE DIES OF OVERDOSE

Teddy Freeman's graduation picture was plastered on the front page. Beneath it was a long obituary stating everything that Teddy had done in his short life. A picture of his grieving parents was on page two. They were weeping and stated they could not understand how their fine son had ever been seduced into taking drugs. The account went on to state that many local teenagers were into drugs and what was the police chief going to do about it – except nothing – which is what he'd been doing since being hired a year ago.

The editorial written by owner, Leasil Leggett, read like this:

We understand Chief Dempsey needs and deserves time off from his duties. We also realize he has recently been through some very trying times and we know he has been back on duty but a short while. Nevertheless, the island has a drug problem among its youth. Time was when the seasonal help drank their beer and occasionally imbibed somewhat too much. The most daring of the seasonals tried dissolving two aspirins in a Coke to get their high. The island could live with that. However, in the past few years the specter of hard drugs on this island has reared its ugly heed. The fact is not only do the seasonals take drugs of all kinds – so do the locals as evidenced by the death of Teddy Freeman a local student, star of the basketball team and son of local business owners and residents Ralph and Esther Freeman.

The fact is drug use on the island is rampant and it is up to our police force to find the source and dry it up. There is no place on this island for killer drugs. A little alcohol is one thing - deadly drugs are another. The island police force starting with Chief Dempsey must meet the challenge. Starting now!

Ira knew Leasil was correct. Thought he could straighten the kids up with words and second chances. He didn't know the Freeman boys were doing drugs, but was not surprised. He'd called on the Freemans, nothing formal, simply a sympathy call. They were distraught. "The Mac", the school's yearbook, had been published late and the Freemans had received a call that it was in. They sent Ned to pick it up. No one in the family had the heart to open it.

That same day Ira walked the nearly one mile to mortician Kirby Kitchen's funeral home,

"Kid had enough cocktail in 'im to kill one of the Grand's Clydesdales. He never had a chance. I'd give him thirty seconds after ingestion."

"Where's it coming from, Kirby?"

"How the hell should I know? That's your job – my job is to embalm 'em. You know I feel sorry for him and his family – but you know I can't take it personal. Death to me is not personal. I'd go crazy if I let this get to me. Everyone who comes in here I know, is – was, a friend of mine – well some were not exactly friends."

A day later Ira asked the Freemans if he could speak to Ned alone – maybe he could get some information from him that the parents couldn't. Ira was more than respectful. They agreed. Ira rode his bike over and he and Ned rode back to the station side by side. Neither spoke but Ira could tell that the death of Teddy was killing Ned – he was suffering. They were identical twins. Both were scheduled to enroll at Vanderbilt in the fall. They even had room assignments and orientation dates scheduled. Life for them was to go to college, find girlfriends, graduate, get jobs, marry, raise families, go back to Mackinac to visit their parents and vacation there – and grow old together. Now, Teddy was dead at the ripe old age of seventeen.

In his office Ira motioned Ned towards a chair and pulled up one beside him,

"I'm sorry about Teddy."

At that Ned lowered his head and started to cry. Tears turned to sobs and Ned's body quivered from his head to his shoes. Ira figured it was the first time Ned had let go. Ira let him sob for several minutes and then leaned over and put his arm around his shoulder. *He's just a kid, just a seventeen year old kid who's lost his brother.*

"Go ahead, buddy, get it off your chest. Let go. I know a little how you feel. I lost my kid sister when she was about your age. Car crash."

This was a lie, as he had no sisters, but Ira had learned long ago that sometimes lies were necessary.

"The only way you can help Teddy now is to help find the pusher. I'm guessing you know."

Ned said nothing.

"Ned, more kids are going to die if we don't put these guys out of business."

Ned spoke low and slow,

"Teddy was the oldest – born over an hour before me. Mom said they thought I might have to be Caesarian. He led – I followed. It was always that way. I didn't follow him with drugs, though. I never took crack or horse – marijuana – yeah, but not the hard stuff. I don't know where Teddy got the stuff. I never asked – he never said. I don't know."

"Well, who'd he hang around?"

"Everyone."

"Well, who'd he hang with that might sell him the stuff?"

"Look, we know everyone on the island – at least the locals. By the end of the season we know most all the seasonals, too. People think we are close and we are – were – but I didn't go everywhere with `im. I did my own thing at times and he did his. I know this – a lot of the stuff is brought over here by the tourists – every day. He could have got it anywhere."

"So, you have no idea where he might have got it."

"None."

"Well, I believe you. But, I'm gonna' find out. C'mon, I'll ride with you back home."

Nearly everyone on the island attended the services at St. Anne's Catholic Church. The Freemans were not Catholic, but that was the only church large enough to seat everyone. In fact the crowd was so great there were two services. In spite of their sophomoric high jinx the twins were held in high esteem by their peers. Many of the islanders recalled when the boys were born, as it had been a difficult delivery. There were not many dry eyes. Juliet who still looked like a ghost attended the first service. They sat together. Ira jotted down the names of all the teenagers who attended – from both services. Over a two week period he interviewed each one. He learned very little. Yes, a lot of marijuana came over on the ferries, via teens, and it was somewhat shared by the locals but there seemed to be little knowledge of the kind of drugs that had killed Teddy. Either these kids knew very little or they were as tight lipped as anyone he'd come in contact with and he couldn't believe they all could be that tight lipped. The Town Crier was no kinder the next week – Leasil Leggett laid into Ira again.

The question is – has Chief Dempsey made any real progress in finding who supplied the fatal dose of drugs to Teddy Freeman? Does he have any suspects? What has been done to prevent the next teenage death? These are not prescription drugs picked out of some parent's medicine cabinet – these are the real deal. We hope for the sake of all island teenagers that.........

Ira read it with displeasure, *I can't wait until October when this thing comes out once a damn month.*

Katy McCormack paid him a visit,

"Any idea where this crap is coming from?"

"Nope, but I aim to find out."

Ira called Doug and Ed into his office and laid out a plan. For the next two days they were to meet every ferry that came into the docks. Ira would take Arnold's, Ed Dickerson would be stationed at Shepler's and Doug Upland would handle the Star Line. They would go aboard every ferry and randomly check backpacks and luggage.

People didn't like it but Ira had the authority and used it. In two days they confiscated four ounces of marijuana – big deal! They laid off a week – they figured the news would get around –and then they started a second search – same procedure. This time they found two bags of very high grade marijuana on a father visiting his daughter who worked at the Marble Creamery. Ira figured he was bringing it to her, but the man protested it was his – so Ira busted him on the spot.

Ira could see they weren't making much headway. He called the police chief down in Detroit, A. C. Drewson,

"Got any extra drug sniffin' dogs you can lend us?"

"Can't lend you any – this town's so broke they can barely pay me, but I can rent you a couple at a decent price. You gotta come get 'em."

"How much?"

"How long do you want 'em for?"

"A week."

"How many?"

"Three."

"I'm sure the frickin' rate's in some manual, but I don't have time to look it up. Thirty bucks each."

"Sold."

Ira sent Officer Upland,

"How in the hell do you expect me to bring back those three mutts?"

"In the car. It does have a steel partition between you and the enemy."

"They'll shit all over the car."

"Then we'll clean it up – it's no worse than a lot of other stuff we find back there. Here's ninety bucks. Get goin'."

Officer Upland muttered and moaned all the way down and back. The dogs barked and bayed and he had to stop at a Walgreens and buy some ear plugs – but they did not have any accidents in the car. He delivered three German Shepherds that had noses like Scaramouch. Ira gave each of the officers a dog and for the next week they sniffed everything on all three ferry lines including the crotches of male and female alike. Upland's dog, Razor, sniffed both Freddie's crotch and back pack. Freddie turned scarlet and tried to push him off his crotch.

"What the hell you got in that back pack, Freddie?" Upland demanded.

"Peanut butter thandwiches! Peanut butter thandwiches! I dot three of them thandwiches. That'th my lunth."

"Well, Freddie, looks like Razor's got a nose for peanut butter – dumb assed dog. And we're supposed to find drugs with these dummies. Probably trained to bite niggers."

They found twelve ounces of Marijuana and a little meth on two kids from Petoskey. They were both over eighteen and Ira arrested them on the spot. He called their parents,

"Possession of marijuana and methadone is a felony in this state. I'm goin' to charge them. The judge'll probably set bail but they're in my jail 'til he does."

Still they found no class-three drugs.

After a week Officer Upland returned the three dogs. Each one crapped as soon as they jumped in the cruiser and he had to smell it all the way down and back. When he got back he just opened the back doors and flushed the whole area out with a hose.

"How long do you think it will take to dry that thing out, Upland?"

"I don't know and I don't give a good damn. I'm not ridin' in that mother the way it is and I'm not gettin' in there with plastic gloves and handling that shit. It's clean now."

Ira had to agree.

July pushed into August. Ira and the two officers aggressively pursued every lead, every angle but they never made a big score – several small busts but nothing big. They took turns on their shifts driving around the island or riding their bikes, looking for any indications of drugs being brought in by boat – they were vigilant – all night stakeouts. Nothing.

Ira was doing his best with what he had to work with. They randomly checked the ferries – the word had gotten out and they found practically nothing. There were fewer instances of drug use of any kind among the seasonals. Things were going along as planned. The annual Music Festival went off without a hitch the second week of August. Everyone loved the Fudge Festival that commenced on the twenty-first. The Town Crier eased up on its criticism of Ira – indicating that the death might have been more isolated than was first thought. Then on the twenty-second, the last night of the Fudge Festival, Ned Freeman broke into the high school gym and climbed one of the ropes left hanging from the physical education class all the way to the top rafter. He tied the rope around his neck and jumped. He fell nearly to the floor before the rope stopped him. When the janitor found him early Monday morning his feet were tip-toeing the highly polished gym floor.

The janitor, Rufus Symington, one of a half dozen blacks who lived on the island, ran the half mile from the school to the station. Rufus was sixty-four. He burst in the door. Officer Dickerson was on duty,

"Deputy man! Deputy man! He's done killed himself – hangin' from a rope like a stole chicken."

Ed Dickerson used the patrol car – lights and siren. He untied Ned and laid him carefully on the floor, the floor no one was allowed to walk on in street shoes. He called Ira who was finishing a breakfast of waffles and little pig sausages – drinking his second cup of coffee and had just lit a cigar – as black as Rufus,

"Chief, you'd best git to the high school as soon as you can." Ira was there within five minutes.

"Oh, for Christ's sake," was all Ira could say.

Leasil Leggett had a field day,

SECOND FREEMAN BOY FOUND DEAD
ISLAND DEADLY FOR TEENAGERS

In slightly over thirty days Ralph and Esther Freeman have lost their entire family. Just last month Teddy Freeman died of an overdose of drugs. No one has been accused of selling the drugs to Freeman, let alone charged. On Monday, Ned, the Freeman's only remaining child, was found hanging in the Mackinac Island High School gymnasium. Foul play is not suspected. What has Chief Dempsey done to stop …….

Well, it was déjà vu. Same church, same time, same pastor, same message, same people, same sobbing and crying. Only differences were the name of the deceased and that Ira jotted down no names – no one made Ned jump. Ira had already been to Kirby Kitchen,

"Clean as a whistle – no drugs, no alcohol."

There was another marked difference – Juliet no longer looked like a ghost at the funeral. She had ridden Lady Blue to the British Dock a half dozen times since the sinking of the Little Sassy. She'd sit on a bench and gaze out at the water that had claimed her sleek and beautiful ketch. She had come to terms with the water. It had taken her boat, Deucey, and almost herself – but not her soul – not her. Lake Michigan did not know who it was dealing with. She vowed the lake would not win – she'd build another ketch – even better than The Sassy – win the race, acquire another dog. She'd win the fight. Just as important she was physically stronger. Long nights of healing rest had sutured her wounds, her muscles, her fatigue. She'd hired a cook to prepare healthy meals – lots of fruits and vegetables – raw and stewed. Not much meat. She'd ridden Lady Blue in the sun of August in brief attire – she was tan and strong.

Ira by contrast was pale, depressed, disgusted, maligned, fatigued – worn out. *And to think I took this job as a retirement gig.*

Two days after the funeral Juliet stopped in the station. She bypassed Janet, as usual, and sat easily in a chair across from his desk. She was wearing very, very, short white shorts with a peach pullover. Not a good choice with her red hair. She had her hair tied back in a ponytail. With her wild red hair it was not your usual ponytail – it looked as if someone had lobbed in a three inch firecracker and it had exploded – it was not chic. Her long legs, made longer by the short shorts were as tanned as a freckled girls legs could be. The freckles ran together and that made the tan. He'd had his head in his hands – rubbing his eyes and didn't see her until he looked up. He was surprised,

"Hi. You look good," he stammered.

"The sun doesn't shine on the same dog's ass every day, but it's been awhile since yours has seen any. I just came from Doud's. I bought two of the biggest rib-eyes you've yet to see. Don't dress up and don't bring anything – that means wine. Eight o'clock – I know – you'll be starving by eight."

Ira was as refreshed when she left as he had been tired before she came. No one could lift his spirits like Juliet and he knew she carried a heavy load. If she could put her losses and problems behind her – he could too – at least for a night. He couldn't wait for the day to end. He actually whistled as he rode his bike to Darlene's. He wanted to take a nap, but he was so excited about seeing Juliet again – other than at funerals – that when he lay down he could hardly sleep.

He was thinking of her when he drifted off. He'd set the clock for six-thirty and when it went off he was still thinking of her – maybe dreaming of her. He showered and shaved in the shower. He always wore boxers and he pulled a pair of brushed jeans over them – soft. It can get cool late in August and he wore a V-neck T-shirt under a long sleeved denim shirt. Put on a pair of black loafers which he kept polished. At seven forty-five he splashed on a bunch of Aramis. It had good staying power. Aramis, well Aramis, was the perfume of the gods as far as Ira was concerned. Believe it or not at one time Ira had been a deacon in his church. This was long ago and as I said now Ira stood just to the right of atheism. Anyway, at one of the meetings he smelled this wonderful fragrance. At last he asked, "Who's wearing that great shaving lotion?" And it turned out to be the pastor of the church. "My wife loves it." Well, it turned out that not only did his wife love it but so did the church secretary, Lorna Woods, with whom the pastor was adulterating.

Juliet was sitting on the front porch step when he rode up. Acey was at her side. Ira was late, the bike chain had slipped off and he had grease all over his hands from putting it back on. She wore a dress. He had never seen her in a dress. It was pale blue – lilac. It was crisp and long and she had it pulled over her knees as she sat. Her head rested on her knees – her red hair hanging down. The bodice was tight and her breasts strained against it. She had on hose and they covered the freckles but let the tan show through. *Hose, this is special.* It was cool and she wore a delicate, white, loose-knit sweater. Her hair, freshly washed and not quite dry, hung in ringlets and rather clung to her face. She smelled of soap – not a trace of perfume. *If angels have red hair, she is one.*

"You smell good," she said, kind of inhaling through her nose and mouth at once. It was sensual the way she opened her mouth.

"You smell better," and he leaned close to her and brushed his cheek next to her ear being careful not to get grease on her.

She started to take his hand, stopped and laughed, "C'mon I've got some stuff to take that off." And she did – a can of Fast Orange. "I go through a can of this stuff a month."

He sat on a stool, his elbows on the counter. She opened the large stainless steel refrigerator door and pulled out a Sam Adams. She didn't open it, just sat it in front of him. He popped the cap and took a deep draft and then another.

"Good," he said.

She set about preparing dinner – not quite as precise as the last time. She sliced two large Idaho's with the skins on, cut up some onions and bell peppers, cut up a stick of butter, wrapped the lot in foil and set it on the grill. Instantly steam started to seep out of the cracks in the foil. She laid the steaks on the grill and started the salad – a very simple salad – hearts of lettuce, some sliced cucumbers and onions – a couple whole radishes. She pulled out four or five kinds of dressings. The whole thing took less than fifteen minutes.

She was correct. He'd never seen bigger steaks – never ate better ones. He was starving. The past month seemed to roll off. He'd never had grilled vegetables. The onions and peppers had just started to blacken on the ends and the potatoes swimming in butter and seasoned with ground pepper and sea salt were outstanding. He was a thousand island man but for the hell of it he tried some French. *What had he been missing?* She served her wonderful Chilean wine and they finished a bottle with their meal. Not a word passed between them – she did talk softly to Acey who sat by her chair. I don't think it took her five minutes to clear the table and put the dirty dishes in the washer.

She took out another bottle of wine,

"Let's take our glasses to the den."

She motioned for him to sit in the great leather couch. He sunk up to his waist – it seemed to envelop him.

It was chilly. The sun was down and it had never really warmed up in the house.

"Would you like a fire?"

"If you would."

"Oh, yes, I would. I'm not used to wearing such light clothing in the evening."

"Well, you certainly had light clothing on this afternoon."

She reddened.

Juliet walked to the fireplace, turned on the gas jets and lit them. She carefully placed four pieces of apple so they'd burn well, but long. The fire instantly flamed. She stood in front to warm herself and was silhouetted by the flame. Ira could see through her dress. She wore no slip and he could see the triangle where her thighs and pelvis joined. He'd seen it once before under very different circumstances – it had little effect on him then – it had a great effect on him now. He could feel it. She moved and sat beside him – close. So close that Acey could not get in between and had to sit on the other side of her – which he was content to do.

"You can smoke a cigar."

"Really?"

"Yes, I don't mind."

"Sure?"

"I'm sure."

Ira pulled one from his shirt pocket and lit it with the Zippo. The Zippo still carried scars from when it had hit the pavement on their first horseback ride. He inhaled – knew he shouldn't – but did anyway. When you inhale a cigar the smoke does not trickle out as it does with a cigarette – it pours out. You could see the smoke as it was silhouetted against the fire – just as Juliet's dress had been.

She poured them a glass of wine.

He took another puff and did not inhale.

She sipped her wine. He took, well – it was almost a gulp.

She doesn't like this cigar. She only said it because of me. I'll bet this is the first tobacco that's ever been smoked in this house. He got up and threw it in the fireplace.

"It's no good," he said.

"Oh." Then, "You know, what you did on the Little Sassy was an heroic thing."

"You think I was gonna' let you die? The hero was Acey."

"I know it. It was all my fault."

"Oh? You can control the weather?"

"I should have never asked you."

"Do you really think I'd let you go by yourself or with someone else."

"I don't know. Would you?"

"No."

"Why not?"

"Because I don't trust you with anyone else – you'd kill him."

"I about killed you."

"I can take care of myself."

"Have you ever seen *Nobody's Fool*?"

"What is it?"

"It's a movie."

"No, I've never seen it."

"The main character reminds me of you – a little. Would you like to see it?"

"If you do."

"It's old. It's on video."

Juliet stood up – Acey jumped off the couch. She walked to the left of the fireplace and laid her hand on a piece of cherry wood. Out of the wall came a case full of videos and DVD's, all alphabetical. She selected the movie and inserted it in the player. She had a flat TV that took up most of the wall to the right of the fireplace. She wasn't certain how many inches it was – she'd never asked. She sat beside him again – closer. Acey to her right. She poured them more wine.

The movie starred Paul Newman, Jessica Tandy, Melanie Griffin, Bruce Willis and Philip Seymour Hoffman.

"There's a scene in here where Melanie Griffin raises her blouse. You have to close your eyes," she said.

"I doubt it." And he didn't.

"And at the very end they're playing poker – maybe strip poker for this one girl, Ruby, is sitting there half naked – so you need to close your eyes again."

He didn't.

They had another glass of Chilean wine.

The last scene showed Sully, played by Paul Newman, fast asleep in a chair – a dead Swisher cigar hanging in his mouth. Miss Beryl, his landlady, played by Jessica Tandy, walked over and took the cigar out of his mouth and put it in an ash tray. The movie ended.

Ira liked it. He didn't think he resembled Sully but if Juliet thought so it was okay, for Sully was one good guy. He didn't get the chance to tell her as he was fast asleep.

"No," she said softly, "This is not when you're supposed to close your eyes." She shook him gently, "Wake up," and she took him by the hand and led him up the spiral staircase. Acey followed.

The bed was not fancy – not opulent. It was not even queen sized. He was wide awake by the time he reached the top. He'd wanted this from the day she first walked in his office with her tight white blouse, jodhpurs, riding boots and her riding cap with the scarf tied to it. He could see her there in his office striking her riding crop hard on her left boot and announcing hotly, "Look, here, if you don't do something with those little Freeman creeps I'm going to stick this crop up their little asses." And now the Freeman twins were gone and they didn't turn out to be creeps, after all. They very well may turn into heroes.

She pulled out his shirttail and unbuttoned his shirt, cuffs first and very slowly – sensuously – top to bottom. Her body near his. She unfastened his belt. His jeans had buttons – no zippers for Ira. She teased each one starting at the top. When she reached the last she could feel him. She knelt before him and pulled his jeans to the floor and took them off his feet.

She stood and came to him. She put both arms high around his neck and kissed him gently on his lips. He kissed back harder– she could feel him through her dress. She smiled – to herself – he was at her navel. *You're a little high.* Then she smiled and he could see it. She was smiling at something Katy McCormack had once said, "A hard man is good to find." *True. True.* She took off his T-shirt and ran her fingers through the hair on his chest – still black and thick at forty-six.

She pulled off the coverlet and dropped it at the end of the bed. Acey lay on it as if he knew he should. Only a sheet remained – light blue, the color of her dress – six hundred stitches per inch. She pulled it back, took Ira by the hand and led him to the side. He lay down and she pulled the sheet above his boxers.

"I'll be back."

She descended the spiral staircase. Ira wondered what she was doing. She came back with two glasses and a full bottle of the Chilean wine she'd been plying him with all night. She placed the glasses and bottle on the night stand. She sat on her edge of the bed and rolled down her hose. They lay in brown puddles. She stood and pulled her long, crisp lilac dress over her head. She had trouble as the bodice was tight and it pulled her hair. She shook her hair and it tumbled down upon her bare shoulders. The vivid red of her hair contrasted with her pale freckled shoulders. Ira had been correct she had no slip on. Her breasts were taut in her soft bra. She folded her dress neatly and hung it over the vanity chair then slipped in beside him.

She nudged him onto his side. She unfastened her bra, slipped out of her panties and snuggled up to him, her arms around his chest, her breasts against his back – he could feel them. He could feel, too, the wild and unruly hair he had seen when he had undressed her on the Little Sassy. It was moist and pressed against his lower back.

She caressed him, ran her fingers through the coarse hair on his chest, played her fingers across his lips and ran her hand below his waist to an even courser body of hair. He trembled. She touched him – she had never touched a man before. She put her hand around it and released – quickly. She knew enough about men to know what a woman's touch could do.

She rolled over to her back and bent her knees up. He rolled over on his other side and caressed her breasts. He placed his mouth upon one breast and sucked gently. She arched her back like a kitten.

He took his hand and stroked that area where the wild red hair grew – it was moist and pliant. She lowered her legs and opened them. She was a beautiful red butterfly leaving the cocoon. He was in between those long legs.

"I'm a virgin."

"I won't hurt you."

"I know that."

And then, "When we were in the raft – what did you say to me?"

He was quiet, "I said I love you."

"I know that."

"And?"

"I love you, too."

He entered her and like a teenager he climaxed. He had been thinking about her for a year. She knew he would – she was not upset. She knew he was going to be with her for the night.

She poured more wine. They drank. They talked. He told her how badly he felt about the Little Sassy,

"I'll build a better one."

He told her how badly he felt about Deucey. "No dog will ever take Deucey's place, but I will have another. Now, I will tell you how bad I feel for you and the Freeman boys."

"You may be able to talk about the Little Sassy and Deucey but I can't talk about the Freemans. All I want to do is make love to you."

She reached down and touched him, more than that, she encircled him and it grew and he was on top and it was longer this time and she arched and shook and coveted each throbbing thrust.

She poured more wine and they did not speak. She caressed him and he her. Then he started to stroke where the wild hair grew – gently and slowly – very gently, very slowly then somewhat faster but just as gentle – she moved that area as only a woman can. His fingers moved a bit faster – she moved more – still gentle – but faster. Faster. Soon his fingers were fairly flying in the wild hair – faster, she moved more – faster – she moved more – faster – faster – faster

– and she could not deny it she arched her back and met him head on. It was minutes before they were done.

"Jesus Christ! What have I been missing?"

They slept.

It was late when they awoke,

"My bike's still down there."

"Give the neighbors something to talk about," and she got out of bed and dressed.

Ira stayed in bed and lit a cigar. It was the sweetest he'd ever smoked.

CHAPTER FIFTEEN

Ira had never felt better – ever. In spite of the flack he was catching from the paper and some of the locals he was on cloud nine – hard for a forty-six year old. Ira was in love – for the first time – ever.

He didn't neglect his duties. He and the deputies kept busy trying to find the sources of drugs on the island. Labor Day was around the corner. He was determined to prevent a large supply of drugs coming in for the holiday. He hired the dogs again for Saturday, Sunday and Monday. Drove down and got them himself – had no trouble. Ira, Ed and Doug slept when they could – otherwise they were on duty. Ira had a plan for the holiday and the week after. They were sticking to it. For three days they were at the docks checking everybody and everything. Not much turned up. The same dog, Razor, went after Freddie's peanut butter sandwiches all three times,

"Damned dog's got a peanut butter fetish," Upland swore.

There were a lot of drunks Labor Day and Labor Day night. The cells were full. The fact that it rained hard right after the fireworks and then a steady drizzle the rest of the evening slowed things down. There was some marijuana – hell, you weren't going to stop it all. Ira thought they'd done a good job. There were few tourists after Monday. The island was closing down. Friday morning it was cold – not cool – cold – in the low forties. Ira was at the top of Cadotte Hill chaining it off. He could see his breath. He put a big-assed chain about halfway down and another at the bottom. They might find another hill to ride their bikes down but it was not going to be Cadotte.

Ira sent Slim Dickerson in the patrol car around the island – three times – looking for beer caches for the Annual-Year-End-Bicycle-Race-Around-The-Island. He found eleven cases – all of it Bud Light except for once case of Miller Lite. Typical twenty year old's beer. Dickerson shook his head,

"You'd think they'd buy some decent beer."

They were still going to have their bon fires and the shirts and skirts would still go up, but Ira reckoned things were going to be better than last year. He was correct. The three of them were very visible, even though it meant going without sleep. But what the hell, in two days the entire island would be asleep. Some bike riders raced down Fort Street. But it is not nearly as steep as Cadotte Hill and no one was seriously injured – well, there was one girl who broke an arm. Ed Dickerson had found eleven cases of beer but there were fourteen out there and the other three cases ended up with the racers, but how far can you go with seventy-two beers and two hundred kids? All in all Ira, Ed and Doug figured they had done well. A collective sigh of relief emitted from all the inhabitants as the last seasonals trooped aboard the ferries Sunday morning. By late afternoon they were gone.

Sunday night Ira visited Juliet. They did not eat, rather they sat by the fireplace and drank Chilean wine. They made love on the plush leather couch and Ira rode his bike home.

Monday morning Ira whistled his way to work. He loved to whistle. It was one of the best things he did. When he walked into the station he thought he was one of the luckiest guys alive. With the leaving of the seasonals, Ira thought there would be little in the way of drug or drinking problems – or so he hoped. He expressed the same to Janet and then said, "You know, Janet, in spite of the Freeman thing and all I love this job. I'm a pretty lucky guy."

"Well, you've got the best woman on the island."

"Yeah, I know that."

Danny Partlow had just turned thirteen. His mother, Joan, was a widow. She made ends meet by working at Nadia's Fashion Shop on commission. She was an excellent saleslady but what she earned barely made it possible for her and Danny to maintain the home she had made with her husband, Roger. Roger was a hunting guide in the UP. He had been guiding three businessmen from Traverse City for moose. The UP is pretty wide open and it is unusual to find a fence row up there – but find one they did. Roger's rule was that all chambers had to be emptied and all weapons on safety while crossing or climbing a fence. One of the party, an insurance agent for Assurance, was either too damned dumb to follow directions or thought he already had. He did have his safety on. Just as the fellow landed on the other side of the fence he stumbled on a branch and his little finger just brushed the safety and slipped it off. The thud of his foot coming down discharged the thirty-aught-thirty and the bullet ripped through Roger's femoral artery. When he fell his head hit a fallen tree by the fence row and he was unconscious. Now, the businessmen knew nothing about first aid and lost their heads. All they would have needed to do was put pressure on the wound. Instead they tried to carry him out and Roger bled to death before they got him a hundred yards.

To help his mother out Danny worked at The Harrisonville General Store as a delivery boy. That is to say he delivered goods to the islanders, mostly groceries. This service had been standard practice for years. Katy McCormack had been a customer of Harrisonville's for over twenty years. Each Saturday morning she called in her order and sometime before the day was done young Danny would deliver it. If the order was small he'd place it in the basket on his bike. If the order was large he'd put it in a wooden wagon (the wagon had been part of Harrisonville's since 1947) along with other orders and pull it with his bike.

Mayor Katy had called in Saturday but because of the holiday Danny had so many deliveries he had failed to get Katy's to her. John Maynard, the owner of Harrisonville's, called Katy and said they'd be delivered first thing Monday morning. She was a little miffed as she wanted to make some lamb chops on Sunday, but said it was okay.

Danny's first delivery Monday was to Katy's house on Cow Path. That's what it was called – it was not Cow Path Street or Road or Avenue – just Cow Path. It was cold Monday morning and Danny had his coat and hat on. All of it was uphill and he was pulling the wagon. He was whipped when he got there. The door was open, more than partway. Danny rang the bell, but got no answer. He rang it again with the same results – rang it again – nothing. He yelled a couple times. There was no answer. He thought about leaving the groceries on the porch but knew he shouldn't so he turned his bike around and went back to the store,

"Did she give you a good tip?" John asked.

"She wasn't home. I knocked two or three times and hollered once or twice, but nobody answered. The door was open but I didn't think you'd want me to leave the stuff on the porch."

"No, I wouldn't, but you can go back up there and if the door is still open you can put the perishables in the refrigerator and leave the rest on the kitchen table. So go do it."

Well that ticked Danny a little. It was a hard pump up that hill and the wooden wagon which had wooden sides was filled all the way up and was hard to pull. So, he'd have to pump there, put the groceries away and get no tip. So, yes, he was a little ticked.

Nevertheless, Danny did it – he knew how much his mother depended on the money he earned. Actually, Danny got to keep the money, but it was just that much less his mother had to spend on things he wanted or needed. So, up he went.

Nothing had changed, the door was still ajar and it was dark inside. He knocked and hallooed a couple of times – no response. He walked in and from the porch you enter right into the kitchen. He opened the refrigerator. There were more cans of beer and bottles of wine than anything else. *Woman's a wino*, Danny thought. He put the fruit and vegetables in the crisper and the milk on the top shelf. There was a ten pound bag of potatoes that he put in the bottom drawer. The meat went into the freezer. This was not the first time he'd done this kind of thing and he did it at home all the time. Done. He looked around to see if he'd missed anything and saw some goo on the kitchen linoleum near the living room door. It was kind of brown. Danny stuck a finger in and looked. *What the hell is this?* Wiped it on his pants – looked some more. The brown goo was like a trail – into the living room. He followed the trail. Looked. What he saw made him freeze in his tracks,

"Jesus Christ!" and he jumped on his bike. He had still a small order of groceries for Mabel Dorsett who lived on Valley Road, the road that ran parallel to Cow Path.

The order was mainly of canned goods and nonperishables. Most of it bounced out of the wagon as he careened madly for – where *was* he to go? Cow Path was strewn with cans of Progresso soups, tuna fish, sardines, salmon, wheat thins and loafs of bread. A can of Ragu Sauce hit the road and exploded – so did a jar of Clausen pickles. Danny did not care.

He headed straight for the police station. He didn't bother about putting down the kickstand. He slammed the bike down on its side. The wooden wagon, still attached to the bike, flipped over and the remaining groceries rolled toward the door. Danny kicked them out of his way and ran into the station.

"Chief! Chief! Goddamn! Chief! They're all dead! Dead! Dead! Goddamn dead!"

This was right after Ira had told Janet he was he luckiest guy on the island. He'd lit a cigar and was going through a mountain of paperwork he'd neglected since before Labor Day. Danny scared him so much half of it went on the floor.

"What the hell you talkin' about, son. Who's dead? Who the hell are you? Didn't anyone teach you to knock?" Ira was sorry he'd said about knocking – he could tell the kid was agitated.

"The Mayor! The Mayor! The frickin' Mayor! And Freddie! And Freddie, too. Frickin' Freddie's got his throat cut from ear to ear. They're dead as dead can be!"

"Where, boy? What's your name?"

"Danny Partlow. At the house, man! At the house! It's frickin' terrible."

"Stay here. Janet, get this kid's mother."

Ira got his gun out of the safe and ran to the patrol car. He was smart enough not to turn on the siren or lights. He didn't want to draw a crowd, but he wasted little time getting there. He drew his gun before he went in, but he knew only bodies were in the house. His years as a PI did not prepare him for what he saw. He'd read about "bodies in a pool of blood" and it was true. Freddie was on his stomach literally in a pool of blood. Well, it had been a pool – it was dried goo now – dark brown and ugly and it had a smell to it. Someone had given Ira a bowl of duck-blood soup once and it had the same smell. Ira was cautious, damned cautious. He did touch what he thought would be the left carotid artery on Freddie's neck.

He knew there would be no pulse. He didn't want to move anything until he had a chance to see things as they were. He pulled Freddie's head slightly to the right and it just about came off in his hand. Freddie was truly cut from ear to ear.

There in a straight chair sat Mayor Katy McCormack. A heavy black plastic trash bag had been placed over her head and tied tight at her waist with a heavy white cord. Several other pieces of the same cord strapped her to the chair. Her feet were tied to the rungs – same cord – so she could not tip the chair over. Atop the trash bag and presumably over her head sat one of her garish hats. The most bizarre thing, however, was the fact that someone had taken some yellow duct tape and made a yellow "smiley face" right where her face would have been. You could see where Katy had tried to bite through the heavy plastic in order to breathe, but it was too thick to get a purchase with her teeth and she barely made a small hole in it. She had suffocated and she had fouled herself – he could smell it.

He used his cell phone to call Ed Dickerson and Doug Upland,

"Get right over to the Mayor's house. There's been a murder. I've got the squad car."

"Be right there, Chief," said Dickerson.

"Ed, bring the camera, fingerprint kit and something to take a lot of notes on," Ira said before hanging up.

"What the hell, I just got to sleep," said Upland when Ira called.

"I don't give a good goddam. Get your ass over here."

CHAPTER SIXTEEN

Ed Dickerson was there in a matter of minutes. It took Doug Upland nearly a half hour to arrive – still yawning,

"Well, I had to shower. I always shower when I get out of bed."

In the meantime Ira and Ed Dickerson had put yellow crime-scene tape all around the house. A crowd was beginning to form. Danny Partlow had picked up his bike along with the spilled groceries and raced back to Harrisonville's where he breathlessly informed John Maynard of what he had seen,

"There's blood all over the place."

John Maynard in turn phoned Leasil Leggett,

"Leasil, have you heard about Katy McCormack and Freddie?"

"No, why?"

"They're dead."

"Dead? What do you mean dead?"

"Just that. The boy, here, took her order of groceries up this morning and they're both dead. Murdered."

"What makes you think they were murdered?"

"Well, Freddie's got his throat cut and Katy – well, Katy was tied to a chair with a bag over her head. I guess it *could* be a murder – suicide."

"Jesus Christ! I'll get right up there."

And he did – along with a throng of other people. It is an island and news travels fast.

Ira waited until Doug Upland arrived before they went into the house. They dusted the front door knob but they thought it would do little good. Danny Partlow had slammed it hard when he left. They made a chalk outline of Freddie's body. This was hard as a great deal of his body was surrounded by blood and he was laying in it. He still had his backpack on. Ed Dickerson used a hankie on the zipper. Three peanut butter sandwiches.

"That dumb-assed sniffin' dog went for Freddie's peanut butter sandwiches every damn time. Sniffed Freddie's crotch and then went after his sandwiches. Freddie turned every shade of red. At the time it was funny as hell. You know Freddie lisped and he kept hollering for the dog to 'Thtay away from my doddamn thandwiches'."

They photographed everything. Dusted everything, even the knots on the cords tied around the plastic bag and around Katy McCormack. They used surgical gloves when they lifted off her hat . They were careful when they took off the plastic bag not to disturb anything. It was ghastly – her head was drooped, but her eyes were wide open, as big as dollars and bugged out. The whites were all bloodshot. It was not pretty. They couldn't raise her head off her chest – rigor mortis had set in. She was wearing a signature dress – white with large red hibiscus flowers – more red than white. *God, there couldn't be an hibiscus within a thousand miles of this place.*

They called Harrisonville's and had Danny Partlow pump his bike up the hill for the third time that day – against his will,

"I don't want to go back up there."

"Well, you've got to," said John Maynard, "The police need to know what you saw."

So he did.

"Tell me what happened when you came up here," Ira said.

"Well, the first time I just rang the doorbell a couple times and yelled in. I could see the door was open but when I didn't get any answer I just left. Mr. Maynard told me to come back up and put the groceries away. I've done it before – lots of times but not here. Anyway, I put things away and was ready to go out the door when I saw this brown stuff on the floor and I stuck my finger in it. It was thick and I said 'What the hell is this?' I went on in the living room and I saw Freddie layin' there and then Miss McCormack's hat and that was enough for me. I got out of here as fast as I could – and that's it."

"Did you see anyone or anything suspicious?" asked Ed Dickerson.

"I didn't wait to see nothin'. I got out of there as fast as I could."

"Okay," Ira said, "I'm sorry you had to go through this."

"Well, this will be the last time I ever put groceries away."

They went back to the investigation. Kirby Kitchen showed up with his hearse,

"Be awhile yet, Kirby. We're still lookin' for things", Ira said and motioned Kirby not to come in yet.

"Well, I didn't like her, I thought she was a piece of fluff, but I'm sorry for this. Damn!"

They took measurements, looked for hairs. There was no sign of sexual assault, just suffocated. No skin under her fingernails. They took DNA swabs of anything they could find. Freddie was sprawled like he didn't know what hit him.

"What do you think, Ed?" Ira didn't bother to ask Doug Upland anything – he watched, though, that Upland didn't mess anything up.

"I think they knew their assailant as there's no sign of a struggle. But how could you kill Freddie and her not fight for her life? They may have had her tied up first. I don't know. I know it was one damn sharp knife that got Freddie – his head's nearly cut off."

"Well, I guess they could have got Freddie first," Ira surmised.

"You said 'they'. Do you think there was more than one?" Ed was wondering.

"Right now I have no idea. I don't think there were many – one or two – from the way things look."

"How smart do you think Freddie was?" Again, Ed was wondering.

"I don't know. I only talked to him once, when I first came here. I saw him a lot but never talked to him. He was always walkin' around with that backpack. What do you mean?"

"I mean do you think he could write? Do you think he could read? Knew numbers?"

"I have no idea. Why?"

"Well, look at his left index finger. It looks as if he's trying to draw the number "one" in his blood. He knew he was dying but he tried to draw this number."

"Oh, I don't think so. I think rigor mortis was setting in and the finger just curled that way."

"Yeah, but by then the blood would have been dried and the finger wouldn't have made the mark. That mark was made when the blood was fresh."

Ed Dickerson lifted up Freddie's left hand. Under it was something that looked very much like the letter "C" – drawn in his own blood.

After spending hours investigating the site and everyone who might have known why this could have happened the only solid clue they had was what looked like the letter "C" and the number "1" that Freddie had scrawled as he lay dying. And no one knew if Freddie even knew what a letter "C" or a number "1" was. For all anyone knew it was a random act.

At about five Ira allowed Kirby Kitchen to take the bodies to the funeral home. By that time the crowd outside had grown to several hundred.

Leasil Leggett had his pad and pencil ready,

"Who're the corpses, Chief?"

"Now just who in the hell do you think, Leasil?"

"Well, we don't know out here. We don't know anything out here. No one's told us anything."

"Well, its Mayor McCormack and her nephew, Freddie."

"How'd they die?"

"I can't comment on that, Leasil."

"The Partlow boy said Freddie had his throat cut and the Mayor had a bag over her head. Is that true?"

"I can't comment on that, Leasil. I can't say anything yet until I've checked things out further."

"Well, when will that be?"

"I should know more in the morning – call me."

With that the three lawmen returned to the house and looked everything over again – again and again. There was no sign of forced entry, nothing scattered about, nothing missing. No bloody footprints as there had been in the Jeffrey MacDonald case. Katy McCormack's purse was there with six crisp one-hundred dollar bills in it like she had withdrawn money to make a large purchase. But, then again, in these days six-hundred dollars is not a great deal of money. Many people carried that kind of money around. Freddie did not have a billfold. The only thing in his pockets were a well used handkerchief and his annual Arnold Line pass that made it possible for him to go into town each day and walk up and down the streets – saying "Hi" to anyone and talking to anyone who would listen to his patter.

120

Ira didn't have much of an appetite, but Darlene fixed him a BLT and a piece of ripe cantaloupe. This was one of his favorites and she knew it. As tired and upset as he was it was welcome. He smoked a cigar and she chain smoked with him. Neither said much and she did not ask questions.

"Tell me, Darlene, who would want to kill Katy McCormack?"

"Well, she could get on your nerves at times, but not enough to kill her. And Freddie, well he didn't have a mean bone in his body."

Ira walked to Kirby Kitchen's. He was just finishing with Katy McCormack. Ira was embarrassed to look at her naked. It didn't seem right. She was his boss – she hired him. The long dresses had served her well. Her body was lily white – save for the freckles, though she did not have nearly as many as Juliet. Ira did not know how old she was but figured around sixty. He couldn't help but think she did not look bad for sixty.

"Not a mark on her body, except where she was tied up. She tried hard to get out. Of course she couldn't. She was tied up too tightly. Tough rope. You'd have a hard time cutting it with a knife. Look here," and Kirby took a piece of the cord and tried to cut it with his Swiss knife – a good knife. Just sawed on it – took a long time to cut it, "Guy had a sharp knife whoever cut these ropes. I haven't started on Freddie yet. Gonna' have a hard time makin' him look good. I'll have to stuff something in there and sew him up – put a high collar shirt on him – otherwise there's not a mark on him."

"Let me know if you find anything funny."

"Okay."

The next morning Leasil Leggett was waiting at the door when Ira arrived – it was six,

"I thought I said to call me."

"Well, Chief, it's hard to get things straight over the phone."

"Can't you write and hold a damn phone? C'mon in, let's get this over with."

"What can you tell me, Chief?"

"Well I can tell you two people are dead, the Mayor and Freddie. Katy suffocated and Freddie died from loss of blood due to a neck wound. There was no sign of sexual assault. There was no forced entry. The neighbors saw and heard nothing, but then cars don't drive up and down here so it's not unusual for people to be about walking or riding a bike. Nothin' seemed to be missing and I doubt if robbery was a motive.

"Myself and officers Dickerson and Upland have conducted a thorough examination of the scene and a thorough investigation to this point. There are some things I cannot divulge but at this time there are no known suspects."

"Any idea of a motive?"

"None. Who would want to harm Katy? Everyone who knew her loved her. And Freddie, well, Freddie wouldn't hurt a fly."

"What's the next step, Chief?"

"Back to square one and just keep working. Now I gotta' get back to work so excuse me." And Ira stood up.

By then Janet was in her office. He called her on the intercom, "Don't give me any calls and above all don't let anyone in here," and he got up and locked his door.

He lit a cigar, took out a legal pad and began to jot down ideas, thinking frantically.

(1) If it's a number it could be anything from C1 to C19 to C119 to C1119. (2) If it's letters could be: CB, CD, CE, CF, CH, CI, CK, CL, CM, CN, CP, CR, CT –anything with a straight line. So how many words do you know that start with CB,CD, CF, CK, CM, CN, CP or CT? Very damned few, to none. How many words do you know that start with: CE, CH, CI, CL? A lot – hundreds, thousands. He looked in his pocket dictionary – there were five pages of CE's, fourteen pages of CH's, three pages of CI's and six pages of CL's. (3) Was Freddie trying to abbreviate something? I don't think so. I don't think Freddie was that smart. I think he was trying to write a word. What is the word? (4) It would be a word that is associated with Katy or this island. And it would be short or it would be an abbreviation. Damn it, it could be an abbreviation. A man who is dying is not going to write "circumnavigate". He's going to write "cir".Or a short word like "clam." Now, there's a word that is associated with this island.

It didn't take him as long as he thought, but it did take him the rest of the day. He went through every word in the dictionary that started with CE, CH, CI and CL. He wrote down everyone that made sense to him. Out of CE he had: cedar, celebrate, celebrity, center and ceramic. From CH he had: chain, chair, chaise (he didn't think Freddie knew what a chaise was), channel, chaplain, Charles, chase, chart, charter, check, chef, chief, child, chime, chin, choke, chop and church. CI's were: cider, cigar, cinema, circle, cistern and city. CL's: clam, class, claw, clay, cleat, clerk, clip, clock, close, closet, clown and club.

That was it. He had looked at so many words his eyes felt like two cesspools and he had a splitting headache. He'd never had a migraine that he knew of, but he could imagine that was what one felt like. He walked home just to get the fresh air. He didn't even take his shoes off – just fell on his bed. *All those words and none of them are probably even in the least way associated with their deaths.*

He lay there until dark and that is late in Mackinac in early September. Darlene knocked on his door,

"I've got a Pabst out here for you."

"Darlene, I couldn't drink a Pabst if my life depended on it."

"Okay, I thought I'd ask."

Ira fell asleep with his clothes on and they were still on in the morning.

The headlines on the Town Crier took up the whole front page. They were in seventy-two point. That's as big as it gets.

MAYOR AND NEPHEW MURDERED
ISLAND UNSAFE?
CHIEF HAS NO SUSPECTS

Sometime after one p.m. Saturday, September 10, Mayor Kathyrn "Katy" McCormack and her nephew Fred "Freddie" Casperson were viciously murdered. This is the fourth death of major consequence in the past six weeks. People die on Mackinac but not in this fashion. It is presumed that Mayor McCormack was alive until 1 p.m. in the afternoon of the 10th as she called in her weekly order of groceries to Harrisonville's, according to the records of owner John Maynard. Because of the holiday Harrisonville's was backed up and her order was not delivered until Monday morning where the bodies were discovered by delivery boy, Daniel Partlow. Chief Ira Dempsey

> *said there was no sign of forced entry and at this time*
> *there are no suspects.*
>
> *The overriding question is what effect this spate of*
> *deaths will have on tourism next season as..........*

Leasil Leggett was correct – Ira had no suspects. He'd narrowed his list of words that Freddie may have been trying to write in his death throes to: cedar, celebrity, center, chain, chair, channel, charter, check, chef, church, cigar (that would point mainly to him), circle, city, clam, cleat, clerk, clock, close, closet and clown. Twenty words.

Cedar: well there were cedar trees on the island. Celebrity: plenty of those in town. I don't know any who'd want to kill the pair. Center: the town center and the rec center. Chain: well it didn't look like he'd been hit with a chain. Chair: well, Mayor Katy was killed in one so it might not be a bad idea to look it over very carefully. Channel: lots of those on Mackinac and it would pay to check each one – what for, I do not know. Charter: that is one of the most used words on the island – charter boat, charter this, charter that. Check: a bad one, a stolen one, an owed one. Chef: there were dozens on the island. They floated from place to place except the very good to great ones who stayed in the same place like the Grand. Most of them were pissed off at somebody and some were pissed off at everybody. I'm not certain they're killers. Church: several in town – could be a connection. Worth thinking about. Cigar: that's me and I did not do it. Circle: well there's a word that could mean something. City: that could be Mackinaw City or downtown here. Clam: every restaurant offers clams – how would they fit in? Cleat: all boats and docks on this island have them. I don't think that was the weapon. I think a very sharp knife was. Clerk: more clerks on this island than about anything. Could be, I guess. Clock: an intriguing word in this instance – something in a clock? Close: the killer is close? Closet: the killer had been in a closet or go look in the closets – the clues are there. Clown: clowns were part of the island. Was the guy in a clown suit? That was it for the moment.

Ira called Slim Dickerson and Doug Upland in for a brain storming session. It was a misnomer in the case of Upland. He was upset for having to come in on his day off. Ira gave them his list of words and they went over and over them. They were at it for nearly three hours. They drew mostly blanks. They dismissed most of the words. They spent more time on: *chain, chair, channel, charter, check, chef, clock and closet* than any others. Doug Upland probably nailed it when he said,

"Nobody knows what the hell old Freddie was trying to say, if anything. It might have been "Eye See" or "See I" or not a damned thing. It's a frickin' needle in a haystack."

The funeral was held in St. Ignace at the Lutheran Church. Even St. Anne's was not large enough to handle the expected crowds who wanted to pay their last respects to Kathyrn "Katy" McCormack, deceased mayor of Mackinac Island. In November she would have completed thirty-six years of being the most important political figure on the island. She was laid out in what would have been typical attire had she been living – a long bright blue dress with orchids in white silhouette, white shoes and a hat that would have looked out of place anywhere but there. One hundred fifty-nine mayors from villages, towns and cities in the state of Michigan attended. Clyde Stone gave one eulogy and said,

"I saw her every time I came to Mackinac for the past thirty years. Tried to tell her to run the place like I did Kankakee. She never paid any attention. It was all in fun anyway. She was a great lady and my visits here will not be nearly so pleasant without her."

Kirby Kitchen said, "I ran against her seventeen times – never really expected to win, but it provided newsprint and gave Katy something to work towards. She loved to campaign and so did I so we stirred up things on the island. Not much goes on here." It was then Kirby realized what he'd said and hastily added, "At least not until recently. But I have faith in Chief Dempsey, he'll find out who did this."

The next day the island council named Kirby Kitchen interim mayor of Mackinac Island until an election could be held in November. Kirby said, "I'm going to just try and do what Katy would have wanted done, but I'm not going to walk around in wild dresses and hats."

As for Ira he offered no eulogy and he was sick of attending funerals.

Ira interviewed all the neighbors, checked the chair over carefully – nothing. He made a thorough search of every closet. The only things that turned up of any consequence were three porno magazines – mostly girls on girls and Ira couldn't guess if they had been Katy's or Freddie's. They didn't seem relevant so he burned them – perhaps he shouldn't have but he didn't want people to think Katy was a pervert.

There weren't nearly as many real channels on the island as Ira had suspected, but they checked anything that looked like a channel including all the boat docks. They turned up nothing. Ira couldn't figure how a chain could have anything to do with the murders. He didn't dismiss the word but it went way down on the list. He spent a week checking all the charter boats and anything that had a charter in it and, no, Katy had not chartered anything, nor Freddie, and he doubted Freddie had the wherewithal to do it. There were only two banks in town. Katy was loyal, she banked at the Central Savings Bank rather than the First National Bank of St. Ignace. Her checking account was solid, not as large a balance as he thought she might have had. She had not written any large checks to anyone. She had not cashed or deposited any, either. He checked her savings account, also. She had a fair amount of money in it but again no recent large deposits or withdrawals.

He looked at every clock in Katy's house and public clock on the island – there were not a lot of these – each bank had a time and temperature. He couldn't connect them in any way. As far as chef went – well, Freddie was cut with a very sharp instrument – probably a very sharp knife. The cut certainly was neat and professional. It looked as if whoever had slit Freddy's throat had slit a few other things. And chefs are known for keeping their knives good and sharp. He couldn't figure how a chef would enter into the picture, but who knows – he was open to any idea.

The Town Crier was published weekly until mid-September so Leasil only had one more week to put it to him – and he did,

NO PROGRESS IN MURDERS
NO SUSPECTS IN HEINOUS CRIME
POLICE CHIEF HAS MADE NO ARRESTS

Well, that thing only comes out once in October but I bet he puts it out October the first.

Ira was to the point where he had thought so much, so hard and for so long, he could think no more. He hadn't seen Juliet since the murder. He didn't want to make love to her; he wanted companionship from someone he could trust. He called her,

"Tomorrow's my day off and I'm going to take it. I want to spend it with you."

"Love, I can't think of anything I'd rather do. I'll rent a skiff and we'll sail over to one of the islands and have a picnic. The weather's supposed to be good, but we should go in the afternoon when it's warmer. Too cold in the morning."

"What time?"

"If you're here at noon that should be good."

The day was fine. September days on Mackinac can be crisp and clear. It was – cool, also. He walked and took deep breaths, trying to get Katy and Freddie out of his system. That's one thing they were not going to talk about. She had a hamper, large, and tied it to the rack on her bike. They biked down to the docks. The hamper was so heavy she almost fell over twice,

"Here, let me ride yours and you ride mine."

Well, "mine" was "hers", too. She had three or four bikes in her garage. But they exchanged and he was able to get down to the docks,

"What the hell you got in here, girl?" Ira almost demanded when he took the hamper off the rack.

"Wait and see."

Juliet had arranged for a sleek little skiff, white, trimmed with Kelly green. They loaded the hamper, stepped aboard and were off. St. Martin Island, uninhabited and a place for lovers, lies ten nautical miles north of Mackinac. Even with a brisk north wind they were there in forty-five minutes. It was the first time either of them had been on a boat since the sinking of the Little Sassy.

There are no docks at St Martin, you just run the boat on shore – which is not easy since much of the shore is rocky, but Juliet had been there dozens of times and knew just where to land. They had to climb out and drag the skiff ashore. They rolled up their pants and took off their shoes but they still got wet. Ira went back and got the hamper,

"What the hell you got in this thing and how far do I have to carry it?"

"Like I said, wait and see. Quit complaining. It's not far. I know the perfect place."

Not far was about fifty yards in and fifty yards up, but it was worth the climb. There was a twenty-foot clearing that lead to a rock formation and the whole thing overlooked St. Martin Bay. The view was dramatic. A large pine tree at the rear of the clearing added shade on a hot day. It was not hot, but the sun was shining brightly and the winds, while brisk, were temperate. A smaller pine tree to the north of the clearing provided a bit of a windbreak.

"When I was a girl and learning to sail my father brought me here for a picnic – it was my reward. It's my favorite place in the world. I've come here many times by myself, especially after Daddy died. I've never shared it with anyone else – ever."

"It's beautiful. I can see why you came here. I'm privileged that you would share it with me."

"This place is good for the soul and if anyone needs this place it's you. C'mon, help me unpack."

Ira soon learned what was in the hamper. A blue and gray wool stadium blanket which was going to feel good on that kind of day,

"Here, help me spread it out."

He did. It was large – plenty of room to lie on.

She had packed real china and silverware – *no wonder the damned thing was so heavy* – linen tablecloth and napkins, too. Wine glasses wrapped in bubble wrap. And then the food,

"I made the potato salad."

It was yellow from mustard and had sliced boiled eggs on top.

"Potato salad's one of my favorite things."

"I guessed."

Clausen pickles, Mikesells potato chips – made in Dayton with peanut oil – she had them sent from the factory – a box at a time. Can't find them in Michigan.

"Best potato chips in the world."

Green onions – whew! – black olives, caviar from Romania, crackers, two thinly-sliced roast beef sandwiches on homemade bread from Martha's Bakery – each slice the size of Ira's hand. They were for Ira – she'd made a peanut butter, tomato and mayonnaise sandwich for herself. And brought a bottle of Merlot.

Sailing and crisp weather had given them an appetite plus it was going on two o'clock and neither had eaten since breakfast and that was coffee. They were hungry. They didn't talk much and Juliet kept the wine glasses at least half full. They gathered things up and lay on the blanket, holding hands and looking at the great cumulus clouds that form nearly every afternoon when it's sunny. One they agreed was an elephant, another a deer, another the Little Sassy and then they didn't make any more things. The wine bottle was empty. They were sheltered and the sun was strong – they napped. They awakened. They made love – long and slow, the sun shining on their naked bodies. They were satisfied.

They gathered everything. Juliet took the blanket they'd made love on and folded it slowly and placed it on top. The hamper was much lighter on the way down.

They were quiet on the way back, the wind whistling through the sails and lines made conversation difficult anyway, but out of the blue he asked,

"Why the peanut butter when you could have had roast beef?"

"Peanut butter, mayonnaise and tomato is my favorite sandwich of all times."

"I swore I wasn't going to say anything about the case but when you were eating that peanut butter sandwich all I could think of was something Upland had said. He said, 'That dumb assed sniffin' dog went for Freddie's peanut butter sandwiches every damn time'. Three times that dog sniffed Freddie's peanut butter sandwiches. While you ate your sandwich I could just see that dog sniffing your sandwich. That dog must have liked peanut butter."

Juliet was quiet – said nothing in reply. Ira could tell she was thinking. He had figured she'd laugh over the thought of the dog sniffing her peanut butter sandwich.

"Where were the sandwiches?"

"In his backpack, like always. Freddie always took peanut butter sandwiches into town every day. He went to town every day. Walked all over town."

"I know that. Ira, think of what you just said. The dog sniffed Freddie's backpack all three times."

"And? The dog liked peanut butter sandwiches."

"The dog's not stupid, Upland's stupid. The dog isn't trained to go after peanut butter. That dog doesn't give a good damn about peanut butter – he's trained to go after drugs."

"You think there were drugs in Freddie's backpack."

"The dog sure did."

"Aw, not Freddie."

"Well, you're the detective."

It was late when they docked,

"I hate to do this to you, babe, but do you think you can make it home alone. You've got me thinking. I want to go to the station."

"I've read about this kind of thing. Boy takes advantage of girl and then ......"

Ira protested.

"I'm kidding, I'm kidding. I'd be disappointed in you if you didn't. I can manage just fine – you should know that."

Ira pedaled to the station. Freddie's backpack was locked in the safe as evidence. He took it out and opened it. It was empty, no peanut butter sandwiches. He smelled it – nothing.

Early the next morning Ira was on the phone to A.C. Drewson in Detroit,

"Are you there all day today?"

"I am."

"You got the dogs there, the ones we borrowed?"

"I do."

"Well, I don't want to rent them I just want to see them. I'm on my way."

"What's this all about?"

"Tell you when I get there."

Ira had the cruiser on the eight o'clock ferry and was in Detroit by eleven. He used his lights and sirens when he had to.

"What's this all about?" A. C. asked again.

Ira told him. Ira wore the back pack. They got Razor out of the kennel. He went immediately to the back pack – didn't even stop to sniff Ira's crotch. A.C brought in the other two dogs – one at a time. Same thing.

"Seems there must have been drugs in that back pack," stated A.C.

"Seems you're correct."

When he returned to Mackinac he called both officers in,

"Peanut butter sandwiches weren't the only thing Freddie had in that backpack. Each dog down there sniffed it for drugs...."

CHAPTER SEVENTEEN

So, Freddie had drugs in his back pack – what were they to make of that? Was he taking them, selling them, pushing them, giving them to someone else? Who? What? Where? When? Why? How? How was Katy involved? Was Freddie getting them for her? No wonder she was so damned happy all the time.

The police department had not stopped because of Freddie's and Katy's deaths. Other things were happening. Someone broke into the liquor store and took forty cartons of cigarettes and a case of Absolute. Ira had a good idea who had pulled that one off. It was a certain thing that arrests or non-arrests concerning drugs of any kind were down since Katy's and Freddie's demises. Was that because everyone was scared? Was it because the season was over and the locals weren't into drugs? Well, we know the locals were into drugs. Just ask Mr. and Mrs. Freeman.

Ira went back to the "C's" again. He didn't even know if that had anything to do with anything, but he was grasping at straws and a dying Freddie had given him a straw – or had he.

What did they know? Katy was suffocated – with a heavy plastic bag and a silly face on it – *who would take the time or have the imagination. Guy was weird.* Freddie was almost decapitated. *Sharp damn knife.* The very thick and heavy cords, that had bound Katy, had been cut easily while Kirby Kitchen had sawed on them with his Swiss knife, which is not a bad knife – they hold their edge.

So, who has the sharpest knives in town? The chefs. A knife can never be too sharp for a chef. They carry their knives back and forth to and from work – in a special kit. No one touches their knives – they keep them razor sharp. Who would have the sharpest and best knives on the island? The chefs at the Grand. There were several of them. Which chef had held a very sharp butcher knife to the jugular vein of some poor kitchen flunky all the while screaming, "Theese imbecile has ruined my broths, ruined it completely and I need eet now. Now! And eet is ruined. You stupid little conch. I should kill you."? Chef Henri Petri – that's who.

The next day was Ira's day off. *No more days off until we solve this case.*

Ira got to the office just after Janet arrived. Upland was eating doughnuts but at least he was not sprawled all over his desk – he was sitting up straight and his desk was neat – except for a few crumbs from the doughnuts,

"Wouldn't catch me in here on my day off."

"Oh, but I will. Days off are going to be a thing of the past until we find out who killed Katy and Freddie."

"Oh, for Christ's sake."

"Janet, get Mr. Eddington on the phone. See if you can line up and appointment sometime today for me." Samuel Lee Eddington was the manager of the Grand Hotel. The Grand had a dozen employees with the word "manager" somewhere in their title but Samuel Lee Eddington was "the manager".

Samuel Lee had signed on to be a bar porter at the Grand when he was eighteen. After three weeks the bar tender at Samuel Lee's station quit – just quit and went home. Samuel Lee became the bar tender the next day. In Michigan you can have such a job when you are eighteen. You can serve it but can't drink it. Did such a good job they offered him the same job the following summer. He had a job there all through college. He majored in hotel management at Eastern Michigan and when he graduated was hired at the Grand as the Assistant Room Manager. What he did was to see that the rooms were clean and make certain the guests were happy. Was the mattress fine? The towels clean? Fresh flowers in each room? How was everything in the bathroom? A thankless job which paid very little, but it did have its perks – mainly screwing the college girls who were the chambermaids and also eating free meals at the Grand. But that had been thirty years ago. He'd married Peg Nolan, one of those chambermaids. They had two girls. One of them, Megan, had dated Ned Freeman off an on and she took his death pretty hard, but there were signs she was coming out of her depression. The other daughter,

Sam, was still in middle school and had a smile that could knock your socks off.

Over the years Samuel Lee had moved up through the ranks and eventually was named, Manager. He made excellent money, but then he had the most responsible job on the island. They lived at the Grand in a suite on the top floor. Each daughter had her own bedroom and it was all very private and rent free. Samuel Lee was frugal. They were pillars of Mackinac. Over the years he had been chairman of various committees and sat on the board of both banks – some people thought that was strange. He gave a large sum of money each year to the island's United Way – though not that many people were in need.

He was short and slender with large hands. He was bald and lately had begun shaving his head.

Janet had been able to make an appointment,

"He can see you right after lunch."

"When's lunch?"

"Well, it goes until two, I'd say be there at two-thirty."

Ira left the station at ten after and at two-thirty was seated in the elegant outer office of Samuel Lee Eddington.

He didn't have to cool his heels long until Miss Pennington, Sam's personal secretary escorted Ira into the deep recesses of Samuel Lee Eddington's office. Joyce Pennington had been one of the chambermaids Samuel had been screwing thirty years ago. Peg who may have suspected something said nothing – and nothing was going on. All that was in the past.

Eddington stood when Ira came in, took Ira's rather good sized hand and engulfed it in his huge paw – squeezed hard and almost made Ira wince, but Ira wouldn't show it. Samuel Lee offered Ira a cordovan-colored leather chair and Ira sank into it,

"Now, Chief Dempsey, what can I do for you?"

"Well, I'd like to speak to Chef Petri."

"That's impossible – I mean it's impossible to speak with him, here. He's been gone since a few days after the Grand closed. He goes down to Florida and chefs at the Gasparilla Inn after we close. Comes back here about a week before we open. Been doing that for a dozen years, I'd say. They love him down there – as do we. Of course like all chefs he can be temperamental at times – and he terrorizes the kitchen but the meals he puts out are superb – I don't know what the Grand would do without him."

"I was afraid he'd be gone. Do you have an address for him?"

"Sure do," and Eddington handed him the Chef's business card, "What do you want to talk to him about."

"Well, I'm not certain. His knives, I think."

"Do you want him to get you some?"

"No, I'd just like to see them and find out where he was on the night the mayor and her nephew were murdered."

"Surely you don't expect Chef Petri!"

"Right now I suspect everybody. What was your biggest problem here at the Grand this past season? I mean with the staff."

"Well, it's usually drinking and fornicating," at the word "fornicating" Eddington reddened. "But this year for some reason there's been lots of drugs. I don't want that to get around, Chief."

"Anything you tell me will be held in the strictest confidence. I give you my word on that."

"Well, the thing is, there were lots of drug use among the staff this year – a lot more than usual. Our suite's on the third floor and a lot of the staff lives up there. I know the smell of marijuana – no one can fool me on that. So, when I smell it I just use my pass key and walk right in. I fire 'em on the spot. But this year I smelled very little marijuana but it seemed to me that half the time half the staff was walking around half stoned. I couldn't prove it of course."

"Did you try drugs tests?"

"Well, that's the thing, we can administer drug tests before we hire them, but once they're here we can't test them – that's the law. If we find them in possession that's another thing, but we never found anything on them – and you can't go searching their rooms. That's the law."

"How about your daughter? How about Megan?"

"Well, you know she hung around that Ned Freeman. Now, we all know Teddy was into drugs, but we never saw any indication that Ned was, nor do we have any proof on Megan. She's probably experimenting, but we have no proof. That's all I can say."

"Well, thanks Mr. Eddington. You've give me something to work on."

"Anytime, Chief."

Ira walked slowly back to the station. He wasn't certain what he had learned. He'd found out that Chef Petri was in Florida at some resort, that the staff at the Grand was into drugs and that Samuel Lee Eddington did not think his daughter was using drugs. Ira wasn't certain, but he supposed she was.

When he got back at the station he pulled up "Gasparilla Inn" on his computer and learned it was in Boca Grande, Florida – at the south end of Charlotte County. Again with the computer he found the name of the Sheriff was Carl "Buck" Starkly. He gave him a call,

"Sheriff's office."

"Yes, this is Ira Dempsey. I'm the police chief on Mackinac Island up in Michigan. Can I speak to Sheriff Starkly?"

"Certainly, sir."

A short pause.

"Starkly here."

"This is Ira Dempsey here. I'm the police chief on Mackinac Island up in Michigan. I've got some questions."

"Fire away."

"Well, what do you know about the Gasparilla Inn?"

"Well, I know I can't afford to stay there. It's for millionaires, mostly. It's old, goes back to the early 1900s. The Bush family stays there. Old George is a great fisherman. When he was president they were down here all the time – for tarpon fishing. When young George was president and his asshole brother was governor of Florida they were down there all he time. The town's neat – Boca Grande's neat. When Katherine Hepburn was alive she used to come down here and ride her bicycle all over the island. Why?"

Ira ignored the "Why".

"Know anything about a Chef Henri Petri?"

"If he's a chef at the Grande I don't know anything about him. Like I say, that place's too rich for my blood."

"Could you hold him 'til I get down there – on some made-up charge?"

"Can't do it. Not that I wouldn't. I could find something to hold him on, but Boca Grande's not in my county. Most of the island is, but the town's in Lee County – and I don't think you'll get any help from that guy – he's a "to the letter man". He ain't gonna' hold nobody for you."

"Well, thanks, Sheriff. I'll give him a call, anyway. What's his name?"

"Puckett. Bud Puckett – he's a character!"

Ira's next call was to Bud Puckett, Sheriff of Lee County, Florida.

"This is Ira Dempsey, police chief of Mackinac. Could I speak to Sheriff Puckett?"

"I'm sorry the sheriff's on vacation. He takes off every year at this time to go tarpon fishing."

"Can I talk to who's next in command?"

"That would be Captain Georgeff, but he's with the Sheriff, they both go at the same time."

"Well, who's in charge?"

"Lieutenant Light, but he's not here right now."

"So, no one's in charge."

"Oh, yes, Lieutenant Light is but as I said he's not here. Anyway, not much goes on this time of the year. Not much happens here in September – 'til all the snow birds come down – that's why everyone takes their vacation now. Mine's next week."

"Thanks," and he hung up.

It was right after he hung up that Ira determined to go to the Gasparilla Inn in Boca Grande in Lee County, Florida, where no one was in charge, to interview Chef Henri Petri.

He approached Juliet with the idea and asked her to go,

"Why?"

"Well, it's a two man job and I need Ed and Doug to stay here. Too much has happened in the past few months. As sure as I'd take one of those guys all hell would break loose up here."

"I'm not a man."

"You know what I mean. It won't cost you a cent."

"Money is not the object."

"If I can get Kirby to okay it, will you?"

At this point Juliet's mind harkened back to her asking Ira to crew on the Chicago to Mackinac race and all that had happened during the race and since – and how much she loved this man – craved him.

"Of course."

When he asked, Kirby had reservations,

138

"What makes you think the chef's involved and what are people going to say with Juliet along? Who's gonna' pay for it?"

"I don't know but I can't find out staying up here. Do you really want me to take the entire police force off the island? I'd take Ed and that would leave Upland here by himself – do you really want me to do that? We've got money. For god's sake two people have been murdered. What's their lives worth – two airline tickets, a rental car and a hotel room?"

"You gonna' stay in the same room?"

"I'll pay for her room?"

"I don't know, Ira, it seems far fetched."

"Humor me."

"All right. What the hell do I have to lose – it's a temporary job anyway."

Just as people who live in the south know very little of what's going on up north and ignore the weather – they'll book a flight into Buffalo when twenty-seven inches of snow are forecast and act surprised when they land *"What the hell is this, nobody said anything about snow."* – people up north fly into Texas when the temperature's forecast to be 112F and the humidity is 99% and say, *"God, is it always this damn hot down here. How do you live down here?"* Well, no, just in August – what did you expect.

The hurricane season officially ends November first but there have been some hellish storms in November – and tornadoes in December. It was now mid-September. A tropical storm warning had been issued for the best part of southern Florida, from the Keys up to Sarasota County.

Ira booked a straight through flight from Detroit to Tampa. He took the Cherokee out of storage. Of course the battery was dead. They traveled light – a carry-on each – they expected to be gone no longer than two days. Ira took a box of black Roi Tans. It was raining hard when they landed; wind was about twenty-five. They had MapQuested right up to the door of the Gasparilla Inn. They had reservations at the Airport Marriott – one room. They rented a Chevy Malibu from Enterprise.

"You know there's a tropical storm warning, don't you?" asked the lady at the car rental desk.

"Well, no," said Ira, "What does that mean?"

"It means a big storm is headed this way. We're not certain what we're gonna' get. Most of it's south of here – the Keys and up some."

"We're goin' to the Gasparilla Inn in Boca Grande. It's in Lee County."

"I've heard of it. I don't know where it is – never been there. I know it's south. Good luck. Don't put the car in harm's way – do you want insurance."

"Yes, that might not be a bad idea."

When they walked to the lot to pick the car up the wind was up to thirty – at least – raining harder.

It was nearly noon when they left the airport. They got on I-275 and headed south. They paid the toll to go over the Skyway Bridge. They didn't know it but theirs was one of the last cars to go through the toll gate. The amber sign, closing the bridge because of high winds, came on. Crossing the Skyway in good weather is a challenge – during windy conditions it is dangerous. By the time Ira, Juliet and the Malibu started up the incline the winds had reached a recorded thirty-five. The wipers could barely clear the windshield.

Ira didn't know why he said it, but he did, "You know about twenty years ago a barge hit this bridge and knocked this span down. A bunch of people died. I remember seeing a picture of it and one guy stopped about a foot before his car would have gone right down into the water."

"For God's sake, Ira," and Juliet was clutching the arm rest with both hands.

Just as they arrived at the top, the bridge moved – you could feel it – see it – like a slight tremble from an earthquake.

"Ira did you feel that? Get the hell off this bridge."

Well, they *were* descending, but it was raining too hard to accelerate. He was going forty and that was as fast as he could safely go. He could see nothing beyond him, not even a taillight and there was no place to pull off. Then suddenly there were taillights and Ira nearly rammed the car ahead – it was going about thirty. He hit the brakes hard, they went into a slight skid but Ira kept control and slowed enough to keep from hitting it. Ira laid back and followed the car down the long incline until they were on level ground. They both gave a sigh of relief but things did not improve, if anything the wind increased and it rained harder. It was raining so hard they nearly missed the south on-ramp to I-75. They almost took the north ramp which would have taken them back to Tampa – that's how hard it was raining. As they neared the Bradenton exit they saw a Cracker Barrel.

Ira said, "Let's stop and get a coffee or some lunch. Maybe it'll get better."

"You'll not get an argument from me."

They both ordered beef stew and got cornbread with it. Ira, black coffee of course , and Juliet, herbal tea.

Ira asked the waitress about the weather further south,

"I don't know. I've been here since six. The only thing I hear is 'black coffee', '#4', 'Where's the honey – it used to be on the table' and 'can we sit over there?'"

A guy wearing a ball cap and a uniform shirt that said "Ray" on it and sitting at a table next to them said, "I just came up from North Port. It's worse down there. The weather service has upgraded this thing to a "hurricane watch". There's talk of evacuation of some of the barrier islands like Manasota Key."

"So, is Little Gasparilla Island considered a barrier Island?" inquired Ira.

"You mean Boca Grande? Yeah, I'd say so, yeah."

"We're headin' that way."

"Well, Mister, I'd say you're headin' the wrong way, but that's your business."

They went to the bathroom, picked up four Andes mints, paid and headed out into the storm. They ran to the car. The wind was worse, but it couldn't rain any harder. As Ira started the car he thought about how when the first Cracker Barrel had opened in Ohio he'd thought some about buying stock in the company. He hadn't and the stock had leveled off. He was kind of glad he hadn't.

MapQuest took him off the interstate at Jacaranda Boulevard. They picked up State Route 776 into Englewood. There was no traffic going in their direction – there was a lot of traffic coming toward them. The wind was howling now – you could hear it through every crack in the car. The rain was nearly horizontal as were many of the palm trees. It was raining so hard it was impossible to see the lines and the road was a solid mass of water. Ira could not tell where the shoulders were. He thought about pulling off, but into or onto what? And it was a certainty the rain was not going to let up.

"Damn," Ira muttered. Juliet was white knuckling the armrest with both hands.

They drove through Englewood – most of the town was deserted. Some people were putting up shutters, the wind tearing at them and threatening to take shutter and man into space. They arrived at the corner of State Routes 776 and 775. MapQuest had them turning south and they thought they had already been heading that way. Merchants Crossing Shopping Center was located there and they wanted to ask directions but the center was closed – boarded up – not a vehicle in the parking lot, save for an old Dodge pickup truck which had refused to start.

Just south on 775 they passed Lemon Bay, the local high school. Obviously school had been let out or canceled. Men were frantically trying to board up the many windows – *an impossible job,* thought Ira. Shortly past the high school they saw a sign that read,

Boca Grande Causeway
15 miles

It was the longest fifteen miles Ira had ever driven. It was black as night. Vehicles streamed toward them, bumper to bumper – no one was traveling their direction. If Ira did not get the message Juliet certainly did,

"We should turn around and go back."

"Go back to what?"

"To Tampa. To the hotel."

"But we're nearly there."

"Nearly to what – certain death?"

"Oh, it's not that bad." And right after he said that they came to a traffic signal and the road that led to the toll bridge and Gasparilla Island. Only there was no signal. It had been blown to the ground and smashed – glass was all over the roadway. They turned and even though they were no more than a hundred feet from the toll booth they could not see it until they were practically beside it. Ira rolled down the window. He was immediately drenched,

"How much is it?" Ira yelled into the storm.

"Well, it's six dollars when you can get on, but you can't get on. Don't you listen to the radio, man? There's a full blown hurricane coming. They're evacuating the island! Don't you see all those cars going north? These are the last cars off the island and I'm joining them. Go up there and turn around," the gate keeper yelled, motioning to a place fifty-feet toward the bridge.

The last cars off the island drove past the toll gate. The gate keeper slammed and locked the door, got in his car and joined the parade. By the time Ira had turned around they were last in line. He had to pee. He'd held it as long as he could. He was forty-six with a slightly enlarged prostate.

"I've got to pee, that's all there is to it. How about you?"

"Ira, if you think I'm going to get out of this car in this storm and pee you need to have your head examined. I'll pee in this car first."

Ira got out and peed. He was at least smart enough to pee downwind. Regardless, when he returned to the car he was soaked. When they turned north, back toward Englewood there was not a vehicle in sight. They were by themselves – alone.

Florida is known for its alligators – that's the mascot of the University of Florida. They've even been found in saltwater, but very seldom. They can almost always be found in brackish water and every freshwater stream, river, lake and pond has at least one. They take delight in catching small pets and children. Natives and long timers in Florida are aware of that and keep their pets and small children safe. It's the tourist and snowbirds who keep the alligators well fed.

Golf courses in Florida are notorious for alligators – there's one in every water hazard. Northern golf courses are plagued with Canadian Geese. Not so in Florida nor do any other birds of size hang around the water hazards on Florida's golf courses. Golfers do not go searching for lost balls in water hazards, either. Under normal circumstances the gators pretty much stay in their own pond. Oh, sometimes they will migrate from pond to pond on the same course. These were not normal circumstances. Wildflower Golf Course which was just up the way from the turnoff to Boca Grande had become one large pond – it was inundated. The alligators were moving at will.

143

It was two such alligators that had wandered onto the road just opposite the entrance into Wildflower. Route 775 was no longer a road but a waterway. The swales had long ago filled up and the standing water on the roadway was at least six inches deep. The gators, each fifteen feet or longer, had decided to stretch themselves across the roadway and wait for a meal.

The rain was coming down so hard and the wind was blowing with such intensity that Ira nearly ran over them before he saw them. When he did see them he pumped his brakes on and off as he would on ice. The car stopped a few feet from them. Ira honked his horn, to no avail. He drove near them and they just backed up a few feet and assumed the position. He drove a little further and they backed a little more and lay across the road. This went on three or four more times. A large queen palm tree came crashing down behind them and fell across the road. They had no retreat.

Looking back Ira realized he should have just ran over them but the words of the lady at the car rental desk came back to him, "Don't put the car in harm's way". And the car would have definitely been in harm's way had he ran over them. He got out – not a good move. They eyed him hungrily.

Florida people understand that an alligator can go forwards with amazing speed, especially if they have not eaten in several days. What they cannot do is go from side to side with any degree of quickness. Therefore, if a Floridian is attacked he will go left or right, but a Yorkie, small child or snowbird will try and outrun them and find that – they can't.

Ira tried to shoo them out of the way. He should have shot them out of the way. They moved a little. He shooed, they moved. This was all very dumb. It was raining so hard Ira could barely see. It was growing darker – if that was possible. The winds were approaching sixty miles an hour. Juliet decided to get out and help – worse move. Those Yankees thought they were shooing chickens. Juliet had no sooner stepped out of the car when the far gator lunged and had her by the left calf dragging her to the swale where he was intent on drowning her and devouring her. The other gator, nearest Ira, went over toward the first to share the meal and grabbed Juliet's dangling right arm.

Juliet screamed. To this day Ira can hear her scream,

"Oh, my God! My God! It's killing me! Do something!" and Ira did. He did what he should have done in the first place. He drew his Glock 9mm and pumped five rounds into each of them. The one that had Juliet's leg sank into the swale taking Juliet with him so that she was under water. The second gator was still on the roadway and clamped hard on Juliet's arm – the only part of her that was not underwater. Ira sloshed as fast as possible to her. He grabbed her limp body and tried to pull her to the surface. She was dead weight and so were the gators. She was dying.

Juliet weighed perhaps one-hundred and ten, each gator two-hundred. The saving grace was that all were in water and somewhat buoyant. Ira struggled to get her head above water – one gator clamped onto her leg, the other on her arm. He pulled the three bodies from the swale to the side of the road and dug his heels into the macadam. What flashed before his eyes was a picture he'd seen of a strong man pulling a locomotive down a track by a rope tied around his waist. *God damn it! If he can do it – I can do it!* Mortgaging strength and days from his future, Ira slowly, ever so slowly but steadily, ever so steadily, moved the whole pile to the middle of the road. He lifted Juliet's face up and pulled her upward so her shoulders and head rested on the torso of the gator that still had her arm clamped. The gators beady eyes were still open in death. Juliet's eyes were closed – in death or unconsciousness. She was not breathing. From the mouth of each gator flowed blood – theirs and hers.

"Oh, Julie, Julie! What have I done? Oh, my God, my God!" he sobbed.

Somewhere, I suppose in the deep recesses of our mind where we visit once, perhaps twice in a lifetime came a summons. Do something for Christ's sake!

And he did. He compressed her chest. Again! Again! Again! He gave her mouth to mouth – his breath of life to her. He did as he'd been trained to for just such an occasion – from those deep, deep places that dwell in our minds, that we do not know exist until such a moment.

A BREATH! YES, A BREATH, YOU'RE GOD DAMNED RIGHT – A BREATH!'

"Oh God, thank you." Ira no longer stood just to the right of an atheist – at that moment he was a believer.

Ira tried to free Juliet's arm and leg. But in their death throes the gators had clamped their victim to the death. Try as he might he could not release their death grips. He ran to the trunk of the car and frantically searched for the lug wrench. He threw out the spare and everything that was on top of it – there! There it was! He raced to her – pale in death – or in life. *I will not let her die.*

He pried the jaws off her leg first and was sickened by what he saw – a mixture of bone, flesh and blood. Blood was throbbing from the wound. He took off his belt and fashioned a tourniquet above the gaping wound. Tied it as tight as tight could be. Next, the arm – again a horrific wound. In spite of all his experiences this made him sick to his stomach and he vomited. He took off his necktie and tied off her arm. He carried her limp and ravished body to the car and gently laid her in the back seat,

"Oh, Julie, forgive me. Forgive me."

Ira jumped in the driver's seat, slammed the door, took out his cell phone, dialed 911, started the car and drove off as fast as he could without sliding off the road or drowning out the engine. Never had he seen such wind and rain – not even when the Little Sassy went down. Juliet was still as death. Was she?

"Operator – what is your emergency?"

Ira tried to speak calmly, but his heart was racing, his mouth dry and his hands shaking like the palm fronds in the storm.

"This is police Chief Ira Dempsey from Mackinac Island, Michigan. I'm headed north on the road that goes from Boca Grande to Englewood – I think 775. I've a badly injured passenger. She's lost a lot of blood, barely breathing and unconscious. She requires immediate, I repeat, immediate assistance. I'm driving a red Chevy Malibu. I'll be driving on the left side of the road if anything gets in my way. I'll have my emergency flashers on and flicking my lights. Start someone immediately."

It was fifteen miles from the causeway to Englewood. Ira could make between twenty-five and thirty and stay on the road. He could not see the road for it was covered now by a foot of water. As the old saying goes – he stayed between the ditches. In spite of all that had occurred since he had seen the last car pull out and head north at the Boca Grande bridge it wasn't long before he caught up with the others. He turned on the flashers, honked his horn and flashed his headlights. The traffic was bumper to bumper making it nearly impossible to pass. Mostly he drove in the left lane. This irritated many people who had no idea what the situation was and thought Ira was trying to get in front of them. Some gave him the finger, many cursed him although Ira could not hear it as everyone had their windows rolled up, but Ira could read their lips and see their faces.

One driver, a real cracker, driving a rusty GMC pickup, who had not evacuated from the plush resort area of Boca Grande but rather from the small fishing village of Placida, a mile or so further south, pulled out and cut him off. Ira didn't have a chance. He pumped his brakes and did all he could to prevent hitting the truck – he was not going into the ditch – he hit the truck – hard. Juliet was thrown from the back seat to the floor and in spite of the seatbelts Ira's head hit the steering wheel hard and raised a large knot on his forehead. Stunned, he sat for a few seconds rubbing his forehead, gathering his senses – he could feel the knot. When Ira regained some thought he jumped out of the car and opened the rear door. He picked Juliet up as carefully as possible and laid her gently on the back seat. Blood was all over Juliet and the inside of the car – on the seat where she'd been laying, on the floor where she had been thrown. Ira ran towards the pickup. The driver, a big old boy in bibs, with long greasy hair but bald on top all held together with a red bandana stood grinning by the side of his truck. He had a five day's growth of beard. The rain stung Ira's face,

"Where in the fuck do you think you're agoin'?"

Ira whipped out his wallet with his badge – plain to see, "I'm a police officer. I have a badly injured woman in the back. Move your truck so I can get by."

"I don't give a fuck if you're the King of England. You got no more rights on this road in this situation than I do. I suggest you git in your fuckin' car and git back in line." Traffic was going around them on both sides – very close to the swales and deep water. No one stopped.

Ira looked at him for a second and then reached in his car and got a full clip of ammunition. He jammed it in the Glock and when he came out he had it pointed at the big fellow,

"Hold on now," said the redneck.

"I'm gonna' give you about five seconds to move that truck away from my car and if you don't I'm gonna' shoot you in both feet, drag your ass over in that swale and push that piece of shit in with you. Now move it to the other side and let me by."

The man did not move,

"One, two, three, four ......"

"Alright, you pig fucker, but I'll see you again."

"I hope so – I really do."

The cracker moved very slowly but got into his truck. Ira had hit the rear quarter panel of the pickup. It was dented in good, but drivable. The bumper on the Malibu was caved in and the hood was sprung three or four inches, but he could drive – which is what he did as fast as possible. One parking light had been broken so the emergency flashers did not work but he flashed his lights and sounded his horn and drivers let him by.

Where's the EMT. Where's the squad. It seemed to take forever, but at long last he saw the red and blue lights of the emergency squad. They met bumper to bumper. Ira jumped out at the same time as the EMT's did,

"She's hurt bad – lost a lot of blood. Do something for God's sake." The rain was coming in horizontal sheets, the wind now at hurricane force tore at their clothing.

The EMT's went right to work, loosened the tourniquets, stuffed bandages in the wounds and started giving her blood. They had her in the ambulance within two minutes and within three were on their way,

"Where you takin' her?"

"To the Englewood hospital. Follow us."

At Merchants Crossing a deputy picked them up. He sandwiched Ira between his cruiser and the ambulance. Within a matter of minutes they were at the emergency entrance. It was raining and blowing so hard that even under the portico the rain drenched the EMTs. They had Juliet out of the ambulance and into the emergency ward in seconds. Even at that she was soaked. They wheeled her into a curtained off cubicle. Ira followed.

"I can't have you in here," the doctor said, "The EMT's versed me before they got here. I've got a lot of work to do. Wait in the waiting room. I'll let you know."

That was the last Ira saw of her.

How in the name of God could this happen to us twice? I mean, Jesus Christ!

Ira was relieved when he saw the doctor. He knew in Florida there are a lot of Indian and Hispanic doctors. Not that Ira didn't think they knew what they were doing. He just wanted one he could understand. The Englewood hospital is not large – nothing like Venice or Sarasota. They would have evacuated her by air to Tampa but nothing was flying in that storm.

Dr. Richard Florian was single. He lived for surgery. He read everything he could about medicine. He was up on the latest surgery procedures. He could have practiced anywhere he wanted. Where he wanted was some small town where the weather was good and the pace slow. He loved to sail. (Wasn't it ironic that he was about to operate on a kindred soul?) He lived with his mother, the widow of Dr. Leslie Florian an esteemed surgeon who had worked himself to an early death at the Rochester Clinic while at the same time living in a city that owned most of the snowfall records in the United States. And that's why they were in Englewood, a town so small that it was not even incorporated. They lived in a modest home on Manasota Key. They owned a lot that went back to Lemon Bay and that's where he kept his ketch, My Fun.

Dr. Richard Florian took one look, *It's going to be damned close.* "Let's get going. More blood!"

Ira could not sit – he paced. He paced for hours – for an eternity. The rain beat against the windows. It was not yet five o'clock but it was as dark as a grave. The place was practically deserted – only a skeleton staff and the patients remained. Ira lit a cigar,

"You can't smoke in here!" an assertive lady behind a glass partition insisted.

"Lady, the only person in this world I give one good damn about is in there fighting for her life. I'm gonna' smoke. I'm a policeman so don't even think about calling security. They've got enough to do with this storm." She didn't say more and he smoked three more cigars that night.

About an hour into the operation all the lights in the hospital went out – all the lights in Englewood went out. And they were out for hours. In a matter of seconds the emergency generators came on and Dr. Richard Florian had a nurse wipe his brow but he missed not a suture.

It was three in the morning when Dr. Richard Florian came out from the cubicle and walked over to Ira who was smoking his fourth cigar,

He smiled and said, "Didn't they tell you that you can't smoke in here?" *He's smiling – he's jokin' around. That's a good sign.*

Then he became serious, "She's going to live. I saved her arm, but it's going to have lots of scars on it. I had to graft skin on it and will have to graft some more. It won't be pretty but she'll have pretty good use of it. I couldn't save the leg – I just couldn't save it – way, way too much damage – just crushed. But I saved the knee joint and she'll be able to be fitted with a prosthesis. They're really good now. And best of all – I think the baby is going to make it – no miscarriage.

"Baby!"

"Yes, baby. She's pregnant – just barely – but she is pregnant. Didn't you know?"

"No."

"And you need to buy the EMT's dinner, they probably saved her life. Between us we gave her five pints."

Ira was barely listening. *Pregnant, she's pregnant.*

"Excuse me, Doctor. I've got to step outside for a minute."

Ira didn't want to go out into the weather but the news that Juliet was going to live, that she had lost a leg and that she was pregnant was more than he could factor. He needed air – to think – where no one was around. He opened the door took three or four steps beyond the door. The big cracker was there,

"I thought you'd be here mother-fucker. I waited for you." And he sucker punched Ira. Ira fell backward like a felled tree. He never knew what hit him, maybe never heard the words. As he fell Ira hit his head on the curb. When the rest of him hit the ground his gun discharged and hit the cracker in the left eye and came out the back of his head. He was dead before he hit the ground. Ira never knew it.

When Ira had pulled the gun on the cracker at the scene of the accident he'd taken off the safety and in all the excitement had forgotten to put it back on. No one heard the shot. Only after Dr. Richard Florian had checked his patient and went looking for Ira did he find the pair. There was no need to take the cracker to the emergency room. He was D.O.A.

When Ira came to he was in a hospital gown, lying in a hospital bed – next to Juliet's bed. For the second time in two months they were sharing a hospital room. *This is getting to be a habit.*

Ira had fourteen stitches in the back of his head and a concussion. His head was pretty much bandaged up and there was a large bandage covering his nose. The doctor was leaning over him,

"Well, I see you're awake." Ira tried to rise. "Take it easy, Chief, you're not going anywhere for a while. What happened out there? I don't understand. You shot some guy. Who do you know down here?"

"I don't know anyone. We had an argument on the way here. He was waitin' for me, I guess. I didn't shoot anyone."

"Oh, yes you did – right in the head. He's dead – some guy from Placida."

"I didn't shoot him."

"Well, your gun did. That's enough talk. You rest, we'll talk more about it later. I fixed your nose."

"What do you mean?"

"Well, the guy knocked it all the way to the right of your face – I straightened it up – had a hell of a time."

"It's been like that for thirty years."

"Well, it's straight now."

Over in the next bed in an induced coma lay Juliet, fighting for her life.

The storm passed through by morning, ended up in DeSoto County and practically obliterated Arcadia. Went right up the Peace River. It never had a name – it came so quickly the weather people never named it. It has been known since as "The No Name Storm". Winds were clocked at eighty-six miles per hour which made it a category one hurricane, but it was never officially named a hurricane. So the insurance companies fought with their insured about the damages. The Sarasota County Sheriff's Department investigated the shooting and called it accidental. It was obvious since Dr. Richard

Florian testified that Ira's gun was still in the holster when he'd found Ira unconscious. Kirby Kitchen called and wanted Ira to come back as soon as possible.

"Hey, Kirby, I was injured in the line of duty. I've got fourteen stitches in the back of my head and a damn concussion. I'll get back to work as soon as I can. And I'm not leaving Juliet – you can have my badge."

"I don't want your badge, I want you."

The Englewood Sun, a daily with all colored comics, ran headlines that read,

ENGLEWOOD SPARED
NO NAME STORM REEKS HAVOC ON GASPARILLA
DESOTO COUNTY SUFFERS HEAVY DAMAGES

A category one hurricane with no name ripped through Lee, Charlotte and DeSoto counties and southern Sarasota County. Heavy damage was done to several homes in Boca Grande. Venerable Gasparilla Inn suffered roof and water damage. Operators of the inn are trying desperately to reopen in time for the influx of tarpon fisherman for the annual Fall Classic Tarpon Tournament. In DeSoto county the roof of the high school gymnasium ....

There was quite some argument at the Sun over the word "reeks". The editor said the word had been misused for generations. He said "reeks" means to "smell bad" and the proper word should be "wrecks" but the publisher said they had been using the word that way since he'd been in the business. People expected it. He won.

Ten days after the surgery Juliet was airlifted to the Mackinac Straits Hospital in St. Ignace. Ira and Juliet had an emotional talk before they moved her,

"It was one of the most stupid things I've ever done – bringing you down here on this trip. I don't know what I was thinking. It's all my fault – I just wanted to be with you – near you."

"Well, if I had it to do over again I'd stay home. But I wanted to come. I wanted to be with you. I have regrets – no one can lose a leg and not have regrets, but I have no regrets about you. But will you want me with one leg? I know women who have mastectomies and they wonder what effect it will have on their men. Let me tell you I'd give up both my breasts to have my leg back."

"Oh, Juliet, the question is will you have stupid me – I'm the cause of it all."

"Well, I'd say we were both dumb, but the dumbest thing I did was to get out of the car."

"You got out to help me."

"Love, you would have done the same for me."

"Yeah, I would have. But that doesn't make it any better. Did you know you were pregnant?"

"Ira, every woman knows when she's pregnant."

"Do you want it?"

"With all my heart."

CHAPTER EIGHTEEN

Ira visited Juliet every day in St. Ignace – on duty or off. Her arm healed well. Can you imagine, Dr. Richard Florian flew up to do the grafting that was needed? The skin around the amputation healed but the stump was sore and sensitive. There would be weeks of rehabilitation before there could be any talk of prosthesis. Ira's wound healed quickly. The stitches were removed by old Doc Romney there on the island. Ira suffered from bad headaches. His nose bothered him. Dr. Richard Florian had to break it to straighten it and Ira wished he'd left it alone, but it was straight. Juliet liked it better and anytime Juliet said something positive about Ira he was happy. He was still remorseful.

The island of course was abuzz with the happenings. Some questioned the logic of Ira taking Juliet with him. But most folks sympathized because of the situation. The Town Crier, published only once in October, but early, really did not blast Ira,

ISLAND ICON BADLY MAULED
BY ALLIGATORS
LONG ROAD TO RECOVERY

Native islander, Juliet Steinbrenner, granddaughter of yacht builder Charlie Steinbrenner was badly mauled by alligators while on a recent trip to Florida. The attack occurred just north of Boca Grande, a well-known resort town on the west coast of Florida, while in the accompaniment of Chief Ira Dempsey. The pair was on official business when ... ...

"You should have taken *us* with you, not some girl," proclaimed Doug Upland. Ed Dickerson was smart enough to say nothing.

Ira was angry – angry with himself for what had happened to Juliet, angry with the cracker who coldcocked him, even if he was dead, and angry at Chef Henri Petri as he suspected he knew a great deal about the murders of Mayor McCormack and Freddie. Through the internet he kept track of the Gasparilla Inn. They were closed two weeks for repairs, but when a business such as the Gasparilla Inn is losing a million dollars in revenue a day it gets fixed in a hurry, especially with the biggest tarpon tournament of the year, The Fall Classic, upcoming. *The day these headaches stop I'm on my way.*

Ira drove down to Sheboygan and returned with a present for Juliet. She cried when she saw it,

"Oh, look at her, how sweet. It is a "her" right? Oh, she's adorable. What is she? I know she's not a Great Dane – that's for certain. I'm going to call her Deucey Too."

"She's a Lab. After our experiences I thought we'd better get a dog that could swim."

Ira had paid one thousand dollars for a pure bred chocolate colored Lab – eight weeks old. The hospital made a bed for it in Juliet's room. It never left her side then or ever.

The Gasparilla Inn reopened two weeks and a day after the no name storm. The big fishing tourney was scheduled for the following week. Anglers from all over the world descended on Boca Grande during these tournaments – many staying at the Gasparilla Inn.

Tarpon fishing is best in the heat of summer, but there is always a run in the early fall – of course the temperature in Boca Grande in the early fall is in the nineties. The Fall Tarpon Classic paid out one hundred thousand dollars to the winner – the entry was ten. It's a catch, weigh, take a picture and release tournament today. Years ago, however, the fish was stuffed and mounted for the winner and a scale was taken off the fish and nailed on the wall in the Pelican Room at the Inn with the weight and date noted on it. There were scores of such scales hanging in the room. Hundreds of boats participate in the Fall Tarpon Classic as well as thousands of tarpons – the tarpon unknowingly – they are only answering the call of instinct – which includes gorging on the crab that are washed in and out of the pass by the strong tides. During tournaments the mouth of Charlotte Harbor is an armada of boats and a cauldron of the massive fish – for a tournament-sized tarpon can weigh two hundred and twenty-five pounds. Tarpon are not the only creatures that come into the pass. Their natural predators, other than the humans who seek to catch them, also migrate to the pass. Sharks – by the hundreds.

The day the headaches ceased Ira booked a flight to Sarasota – he'd had enough of Tampa and the long drive to Boca Grande. The day the headaches ceased just happened to coincide with the first day of the Fall Tarpon Classic. The largest tarpon caught that day weighed in at one-hundred eighty-seven. By Boca Grande standards that was a small fish and with two days to go most islanders and tarpon experts thought a larger catch was certain.

No airlines fly nonstop into Sarasota and after he'd spent layover time in Atlanta it was late afternoon when he arrived. He didn't go to Enterprise this time, considering the condition he'd turned the red Chevy Malibu in. Instead he went to Budget and rented a Honda Accord. He arranged a room at the Best Western Midtown, just south of the classic remains of the old Sarasota High School, built in 1927. He didn't know it but when he walked over to Michaels on East just east of his hotel he had wandered into one of the finest restaurants in Sarasota. One look at the menu prices clued him in, however.

Jesus Christ!

The island was paying for it but he ate lightly. A bowl of seafood chowder and a garden salad. He wasn't hungry, he was impatient. He couldn't wait for tomorrow. He called the Inn,

"Say, I'm a big fan of your Chef Petri. Is he still in charge of dinner?"

"Chef Petri is in charge of the kitchen – completely in charge."

"I understand that but if I go and want to have food that he personally prepared when would it be. Breakfast? Lunch? Dinner?"

"The Inn doesn't do lunch, sir, just breakfast and dinner. Lunch is served at the Gasparilla Club – it's a buffet."

"So, would it be breakfast or dinner?"

"Oh, dinner, sir. Chef Henri is here for every dinner – seven days a week. Would you like to book a reservation?"

"No, not yet. I need to talk with my wife. What time's dinner?"

"Dinner starts at six, sir, and is served until nine."

"Okay, thank you."

"My pleasure."

I'll see the Chef around three.

Walking back from Michaels on East he saw stadium lights behind old Sarasota High. They had long ago built a new high school but the football stadium remained where it had been for fifty years. He walked over. The Sarasota Sailors were playing crosstown rivals, the Riverview Rams. Lately the contests had been one-sided, Riverview having won eight out of the last ten games and six consecutive. It was six bucks and having nothing better to do Ira paid the admission and watched the game. In high school he'd been a fullback at Columbus Central, a downtown school, long shuttered. It was the first high school game he'd seen in years and he enjoyed it immensely – took his mind off Mayor McCormack, Freddie, Juliet and Chef Petri. Sarasota had a great running back named Ford and he carried the Sailors on his back on the way to a 27-21 victory. After the gun sounded the Sarasota people flooded the field. Ira walked back to the motel with a much lighter heart.

He did not sleep well; the good feelings associated with the game soon wore off. He had a hard time going to sleep even though he took a couple of Sleep Wells. He woke several times thinking of what had transpired the last time he was in the area and the tragedy of Juliet losing her leg. He was anxious to confront Chef Henri Petri. He was going to surprise him and see what his reactions were.

At 4:14 a.m. Ira gave up all attempts to sleep. He showered, dressed and walked across the street to the Waffle House. He had no appetite. Black coffee was all he wanted. On his second cup he lit up a Roi Tan – black as tar,

"You can't smoke in here", the all night waitress said. She was over fifty, skinny with dishwater hair and purple lipstick that matched her nail polish. "It's a new law, been in effect a couple of months now."

"Sorry," Ira said. He walked outside and sat on the planter wall. A few vehicles were going up and down U.S. 41 – mostly pickups as the journeymen, up early, started their day.

At six-thirty he checked out, climbed into the Accord and started south. He came to the juncture in Venice where U.S. 41 went west to North Port and where S.R. 776 veered south to Englewood. He recalled the time a few weeks earlier when he'd made the same turn off, when the wind was in a full howl and the rain never ceasing. Even though it promised to be a beautiful Florida late-summer day Ira had a sense of foreboding.

He passed through Englewood. In contrast to the last time he was there the little town was bustling as people headed off to their various destinations. He thought about going over to the hospital, but nixed the idea, *I've seen all of that place I want to.*

It was still early morning as he turned south at Merchants Crossing. He drove slowly past the high school. Kids in their cars were filling up the parking lot. He drove steadily – not slow, but he was in no hurry. He had all day.

He wasn't certain where the altercation with the redneck cracker had occurred. Nor did he recognize the area where the infamous gator episode had unfolded. It was bright and sunny – everything looked different. He didn't want to know where it had happened, anyway.

The traffic signal was up and working as he turned onto the Boca Grande causeway. The same tollgate man was in the booth,

"Do you remember me?" Ira asked. "I was here the night of the big storm. You made me go up and turn around."

"Mister, I made lot of people turn around that night. No, I sure don't remember you."

Ira handed him six dollars, "Can I have a receipt?"

It's seven miles from the toll bridge to Boca Grande. The speed limit is thirty-five and there are speed bumps everywhere. Ira drove the limit. He was in no hurry. It was early. He had all day. He drove down the coast to the lighthouse. Boca Grande was once a shipping port for phosphate. Phosphate was mined up in Polk County and shipped by rail to Boca Grande. The pass was one hundred feet deep in places. Once, ocean going freighters docked there and were loaded with phosphate. From there phosphate was shipped to the far reaches of the globe. Until a few years ago the storage tanks were still there. They're gone and have been replaced by million dollar condos. The lighthouse was there to guide the freighters. Everybody and their brother have been down there to paint it. You can find paintings of it all over the country. He got out and walked around. It was still hot in Florida. He didn't walk long.

On the way to the lighthouse he'd passed The South Beach a restaurant right on the gulf. He stopped on his way back for lunch. Had a grouper sandwich, sweet-potato fries and a Key West – a dark beer. Key lime pie for dessert.

From there he drove back to town. He drove down Banyan Street. Banyan trees line the street and crowd up to the edge of the road. The trees are old – some nearly one hundred. They were hit hard by Hurricane Charlie a few years past but are making a comeback. Many, many tourists have been photographed standing next to or leaning against a giant banyan.

As on edge as he had been at the motel he was as now relaxed. He had a plan and it was unfolding accordingly. He parked and walked the few streets in town. There were lots of high-end shops. He stayed away from them. He did walk into Fugate's which is where the residents shop and the prices are decent. He browsed but did not buy. He looked at his watch – not long now. He walked over to the Loose Caboose and ordered a double-dip butter pecan. When they told them how much – *Jesus Christ, this place ain't cheap.* He sat outside around a glass top table and licked his cone. He looked at his watch – time to go.

To a chef his knives are what tools are to a mechanic or what a bat is to a baseball player. Chefs take special care of them and spend a great deal on them – thousands. They protect them and keep them sharply honed. Chef Henri Petri carried his back and forth to work every day from home. Home was one of the yellow cottages that surrounded the Inn – rent free. Quite a perk, as they rented for several hundred a night. He carried his knives in a stainless steel case and each one was fitted with a plastic jacket to protect it and him. Different chefs prefer different knives. Some prefer J.A. Henckles, others Dexter Russell, still others Messermeister. And there is the old standby Sheffield. Most chefs prefer knives made in Germany. Regardless where they come from they need to be heavy, sharp and balanced. Chef Petri owned noting but J.A. Henckles.

Chef Henri Petri had spent most of the afternoon sharpening his knives. He sharpened them lovingly and slowly. He used a diamond sharpening rod – a steel rod sprinkled with diamond dust to make it hard. He also used a good sized whetstone – course on one side, fine on the other. He kept it in a special wooden holder. He had sharpened a ten-inch, eight-inch and seven-inch chef's knife, a seven-inch paring knife, a smaller paring knife, a cleaver, two filleting knives and two large butcher knives with wooden handles.

He was ready for the day. There were hundreds of fisherman signed up for the Fall Classic Tarpon Tournament and many of them were staying at the Gasparilla Inn. The newly appointed dining room would be crammed with fishermen and their families. It would be a big night. He just hoped no waiter or kitchen help would foul him up. When they did he felt like taking his fillet knife and running it right along the front of their stupid neck. He still had his favorite, his twelve-inch chef's knife to sharpen. He drew it lovingly from his case took off the plastic cover and started slowly working it on the course side of the whetstone.

When Ira pulled in front of the Gasparilla Inn it was 2:55. He walked up the steps to the large wooden porch and crossed it. A very attractive twenty-something girl opened the door and welcomed him.

"Welcome to the Gasparilla, sir," and she smiled – sort of reminded him of the young hostess at the Island House. He thought of her for a moment and then, *Get your mind out of your pants and do your job.* Ira walked in.

"May I help you?" asked the girl at the desk, not half so pretty as the one at the door.

"Yes, where's the dining room?"

"Down this hall and first turn to the left – but it doesn't open until six."

"Yeah, I know. I have an appointment there."

"Oh. Well, it's right down the hall."

"Thanks."

"Oh, you're so very welcome, sir."

Ira walked down the hall on a deep piled green and red runner, turned left and there fifty feet was the entrance to the dining room. One door was open. He walked in. A matronly lady, well dressed, was moving menus around,

"May I help you, sir? The dining room doesn't open until six."

"Yeah, I know. I'm here to see Chef Petri."

"He's in the kitchen."

"Yeah, I know." Ira pulled out his badge. "Take me to him."

"Is there something I can help you with?"

"No, ma'am, there is not. Please take me to him now!"

"Yes, sir, right this way." And she led him as if she were taking him to his table. The dining room was quite large and in good taste. Lots of brown rattan. It was a good walk to the kitchen.

The element of surprise!

She opened one half of the swinging doors. Chef Petri had turned the whetstone over and was now using the fine side, caressing the twelve-inch blade as if he was in love with it. He was whistling La Marseillaise.

"Chef Petri, this gentleman would like to see you." Chef Henri Petri looked up. *Ah, the element of surprise!* There was no doubt Chef Petri was surprised – confused, too, just for a moment. It took him only a second. He picked up his five-hundred dollar, J.A. Henckles twelve-incher he had been caressing only seconds before, grabbed it by the point and sent it whistling toward Ira. Ira was ready, his senses girded. He dodged. Unfortunately the matronly lady did not and the knife buried itself in her abdomen. She fell without a sound. Chef Petri bounded out the back screen door, hopped in a golf cart, and fled over the large, manicured, croquet court. Behind the croquet court lay a channel of brackish water where the Chef kept his powerful Donzi 35 ZR cigarette boat, powered by twin Mercruiser 496 HO's with a combined eight-hundred fifty horsepower.

Ira was right behind him. The place abounded in golf carts and Ira was on one in a hurry. Petri had too much lead on him and, even though Ira was on his tail, the Chef was able to board, throw off the lines, start "The Chef's Special", and pull away from the dock. The powerful motor thrust the boat down the channel creating a wake and ripping boats away from their docks. Their owners came running out of houses and condos shaking their fists at the roaring boat. Ira had his golf cart wide open looking for a boat – any boat. He came to a thing called Whidden's.

As far as Ira could tell Whidden's was a marina – of sorts. It was a rambling structure and didn't look as if it had been painted in a century. The wood siding looked like dirty socks and there was a pen that held two hogs, a goat, and a flock of multicolored chickens. Whidden's hugged an inlet leading out to Charlotte Harbor. It had several docks and a bunch of boats, mostly scraggly, tied up. And a gasoline pump.

Ira stopped the cart, that is he jumped out – the cart kept on rolling – right through the wire fence of the animal pen. Pigs squealed, chickens squawked, feathers flew and the nanny goat deftly jumped into the golf cart seat. Ira raced to the dock.

Homer Pickett was one of the few natives who had stayed on the island after the Yankees moved in and converted "Old Florida" to "No parking! No stopping! No fishing! No jumping from the bridge! No swimming! No camping! And No skinny dipping." Homer was a crabber. That meant he went out every morning – early, set his crab pots and ran them that evening. Homer had just come back, unloaded his catch at Whidden's and was refueling when Ira came racing up,

"This your boat?"

"Yep," as he finished gassing her up and put the hose back.

Ira flashed his badge, "I need your boat."

"Well by God, I do, too."

"I don't have time to explain." Ira pulled his Glock from his waistband and pointed it at Homer. "There's a killer and he's about to get away. Start this thing up."

"Okay, okay. Don't let that thing go off."

Now the crabber, The Evil I, was not a tub but it was no match for the Donzi and the Donzi was out of sight with its throttle open headed for the mouth of Boca Grande Pass.

Doug Rhinehart, Bill Daniels, John Davis, Rich Regula, Marv Weidemier and Ion Georgescu had been poker buddies for twenty years. Only Bill Daniels was a native. The rest were northern imports except for Ion and he was an import from Romania. Ion still had a thick accent and while playing cards when a king showed up he'd call it a "kink", such as the "kink of spades". The other tried to tell him that a kink was what you got in a hose or your neck, but to no avail – it was still a "kink". And he played the best poker – cleaned the others out on more than one occasion.

Bill Daniels was a born fisherman. He'd fished the west coast Florida waters since he was a boy. He owned a small machine shop and fished whenever he could. He owned a twenty-eight foot Four Winns. Like a good son-in-law Bill took his father-in-law with him a lot until he got too sick to go. On several occasions he took his five poker buddies with him. They'd go forty, fifty miles out in the Gulf where they always caught grouper. None of the other five were much good at fishing but Bill always saw to it they caught fish. Instead of fishing himself he'd go around the boat checking their bait, seeing how deep they were fishing and telling them when to pull. They took along some sandwiches, chips and plenty of beer, but Bill never drank more than two. Their lives were in his hands. When they got back to the dock Bill put all the fish in "the pot" fileted them and divided them up. Everyone went home happy.

One evening at the monthly poker game, a few days after a very successful fishing venture, the Romanian said,

"You know, we ought to enter the Fall Tarpon Classic."

"Hell," said Doug Rhineheart, "We don't know that much about fishing – period. And we don't know jack about fishing for tarpon."

"I know, I know, but think of all the fun we'd have and Billy Boy, here, has fished for tarpon. Haven't you?" claimed the Romanian.

"Yeah, a couple of times." He was not enthusiastic.

"It's ten-thousand to enter," chimed in John Davis, who had the least amount of ready cash.

The Romanian was an engineer and a whiz with math, "That's sixteen-hundred and sixty-six dollars each."

Even though Bill Daniels knew his fellow poker players knew little about fishing and their chances of winning were incalculable he'd always wanted to fish in one of the big tarpon tournaments. He had a wife, three kids and while ten-thousand was a lot of money, sixteen-hundred was not bad. He thought he could get that amount around his wife, Honey.

All six were aboard "The Burma Girl", Bill Daniel's boat, that afternoon fishing for tarpon in the Boca Grande Pass as Chef Henri Petri and his powerful Donzi headed their way,

"Why'd you name your boat The Burma Girl?" asked Rich Regula as he popped another beer.

"It's from a poem by Rudyard Kipling – 'By the old Mulmein Pagoda lookin' eastward to the sea – there's a Burma girl asittin' an' I know she waits for me'."

"I didn't know you knew poetry."

"Just because I own a machine shop doesn't mean I'm ignorant. Of course I know poetry" and he went on to recite the entire poem.

"I'm impressed," said the Romanian.

And then Bill recited, "A House by the Side of the Road" by Sam Walter Foss.

"That's enough," growled Marv Weidemier, "You're scarin' away the fuckin' fish with that shit."

Bill Daniels, his motley crew, and The Burma Girl were not the only ones in the pass, there were hundreds. It was nearly impossible to cast a line without it landing on someone else's boat. The pass was rolling in boats and roiling with tarpon. Towards that flotilla roared Chef Henri Petri and his powerful Donzi. This *was* the only way to enter the Gulf of Mexico.

There are scores of beaches from Tampa to Boca Grande. People swim off them year round. Even in February you'll see some dummy from Minnesota in the water. It's probably fifty-seven degrees, but that's warm compared to Ely Lake, even in summer. There are sharks off all the beaches. No one believes it or cares. People on parasails or ultra-lights see them all the time, but no one believes them. Even when the newspapers run pictures in the paper which is rare, because no one wants to scare the tourists, they still go in. There are all kinds of sharks: nurse sharks, sand sharks, hammerheads, great whites – you name it, they are off the beaches and in Boca Grande Pass – especially when the pass is thick with dinner, big dinner – tarpons.

Chef Henri Petri raced on toward the armada, throttle wide open. Boats were jammed in the pass. There was no way around them. Chef Petri started sounding his horn. Now sounding your horn in a boat is different than in a car. One blast means you are going to pass to starboard and two blasts means you are going to pass to port. But there was no way the Chef was going to pass anyone – he was going to have to go through and to go through he was going to have to come to an idle and he knew Chief Dempsey would be following him. He laid on the horn.

"What's that dumb son-of-a-bitch trying to do? Scare all the fish away. The dumb shit." This was Weidemier again. All six had their lines in the water. The Chef and the Donzi raced on. Horn blaring. Everyone looked his way.

Directly behind the Burma Girl was Captain Jeff Hansen and his eight man crew, all experienced tarpon fishers. They were aboard the Mary Ann. The Mary Ann was a forty foot trawler. Captain Hansen and his crew were last year's winner. He kept fifty-thousand because it was his boat and expertise that had landed the hundred grand. Two hours earlier he had caught a two-hundred eighteen pounder and was pretty certain that would be the largest catch of the tournament – though there *was* one day to go. Skilled as Captain Hansen was it took him only fifty-seven minutes to land him. Henri Petri roared on. You could hear his horn blasting inside Fugate's.

Several tarpon had already become shark bait – the sharks were doing okay. One had already consumed a two-hundred forty pounder that would have easily taken first prize.

The Evil I was powered by a two-hundred twenty-five horsepower Yamaha so it would move, but it was built for stability, not speed and it was a couple miles behind the Donzi – and losing ground, although they could see the rooster tail.

"Who we after, policeman?"

"The chef at Gasparilla."

"At the Inn? Whad'he do?"

"If I'm right and I think I am, he killed two people. Is this all faster this thing will go?"

"Damn! Yep, she's wide open – we'll never catch him."

"If you get close enough I'll shoot him."

"In your dreams."

Chef Henri was closing in on the armada. He slowed some, not much – zigged here – zagged there – weaved and wove. He tore through a lot of fishing lines and everyone was yelling and cursing at him,

"You dumb shit."

"What the fuck."

166

The Chef was fortunate and missed several of the boats but luck ran out on him. Captain Hansen looked up from his fishing and saw the Donzi flying – at him. He'd been setting their idling, ready to move to keep up with the tarpon. Henri saw the Mary Ann dead ahead and steered hard to starboard. At the same time Captain Hansen gunned her hard to get out of the way – he also gunned hard to starboard. The Chef saw Hansen's move and steered all starboard to clear – but it didn't happen. Henri Petri caught the Mary Ann's bow right at the railing. He was catapulted like a rock from a slingshot – he went sailing.

In the Burma Girl all eyes turned when they heard the crash. That is all except one pair. Bill Daniels was seriously fishing. He was using a large crab for bait and at that instant he had a strike – a big one. He could feel it. A tarpon's mouth is tough, very tough – it's hard to set the hook. Many times an angler will think he has his hook set and the tarpon will leap high out of the water and "jump it" or spit it out. Bill Daniels set the hook – hard.

"Hot damn, it's a big one."

The tarpon, hurting with the hook deep in its mouth, breached and leaped high out of the water. Directly behind was a nineteen-foot great white shark. It leapt after the tarpon, mouth open, teeth shining.

The five pairs of eyes on the Burma Girl that had looked backwards saw Henri Petri come flying over the Burma Girl's stern, his hair slicked back in the wind, arms and legs flailing. Their eyes followed,

"Jesus Christ, did you see that?" exclaimed Doug Rhinehart.

"Holy shit!" yelled John Davis.

"Oh, my God!" Marv Weidemier screamed.

"See if we can help him!" shouted Rich Regula.

"I've never seen anything like it!" marveled Ion Georgescu

"Yeah, how about that. Ain't she a beaut. Boys, I think we've got us a winner. Yeah, I need help. Get the net!" chortled Bill Daniels, his smile from ear to ear. "Yes, sir, a goddam winner. YAHOO!"

It was only then the other five looked at the fish.

"Didn't you see that guy go sailing over the boat?" the Romanian asked Bill Daniels.

"What guy?"

"Didn't you see that guy go sailing over the boat? He went right into a shark's mouth. Right into it. Didn't you see it? He went right into his mouth. Head first. Right up to his ass. That shark just bit him in half. Look there, look at the blood."

There was some blood but there was no sign of the other half of Chef Henri Petri.

Kippi Schwartz had been taking up space on the Big Three, her husband Zack's twenty-eight foot fishing machine. The Big Three was one boat south of the Mary Ann. Zack lived to fish. He owned a small construction company and rewarded some of his top people annually by inviting them to fish in the Fall Classic. He paid the full ten-thousand dollar entry fee himself. Zack and his crew did not do any serious fishing as they were drunk most of the time. This disgusted Kippi and she did not give a good damn about fishing or the tournament. In fact she'd decided this would be the absolute last time she'd ever do it. She wasn't paying any attention to the fishing – she was messing with her iPhone, but she did hear the roar of Chef Petri's Donzi. Her full attention went to the speeding boat. She witnessed it hit the Mary Ann and she witnessed Chef Henri go sailing in the air. She aimed her iPhone at the flailing figure and started snapping pictures. There were a series of snaps but the one that appeared in newspapers all over America was the one taken the very instant Chef Henri entered the mouth of the giant white. It showed the shark, huge jaws open, and the rear of Chef Henri's torso. The shark had not yet closed down on the Chef. The picture was so clear you could see the Chef's shoe soles. The sunlight played upon the torpedo-shaped creature and made it glisten. It was a sensational shot. Kippi sold the rights to the Englewood Sun for five thousand dollars. Filed for divorce from Zack the following week.

The two occupants of the Evil I were near enough to see and hear the crash – they could not see Henri Petri flying through the air. The Mary Ann was taking on a great deal of water by the time they arrived at the gory site. The bilge pumps were operating but couldn't pump water out as fast as it came in. Several boats came to the Mary Ann's aid and took off Captain Hansen and his crew of eight. One boat tied on to the Mary Ann and tried to tow her to shallow water but she went down before they got more than a couple hundred yards. The towing ship had to part her lines in order not to get dragged down too.

A tarpon – megaflops atlantics – is one of the world's greatest fighting fish. They do not give up easy. This was a big one and it fought with all its strength – for nearly two hours. Bill Daniels was exhausted when he at last landed him. He was drenched with sweat and saltwater. It was indeed a large tarpon.

The Lee County Sheriff's Department was called. They investigated the incident and wanted to know what Ira was doing in Lee County,

"I had reason to believe that Chef Petri may have known something about the death of two residents of Mackinac Island. He fled before I could question him."

"Do you always come this far to talk to a suspect?"

"Well, I called your office a few weeks ago but everyone was out fishing."

There were no more questions. Chef Henri's death was ruled accidental.

Officials canceled the rest of the tournament. Bill Daniels' catch weighed in at two-hundred twenty-seven pounds. It was the largest tarpon caught. They split the prize money six ways. Ion Georgscu quickly calculated in his head,

"That's sixteen-thousand, six-hundred and sixty-six dollars each. The price of poker just went up!"

Homer and Ira cruised back to Whidden's. They didn't talk much. Ira offered Homer one-hundred dollars for gas but he refused,

"Naw, I think he was guilty or he wouldn't have been runnin' away. I think I helped solve a crime. I've got two young'uns – boys – six and four. I tell them a story every night. Boy, will I have something to tell them tonight."

They shook hands and parted company.

Ira was shot. Wanted a beer. He opened what passed for a door into Whidden's. Inside was a cluttered mess. A middle-aged old lady sitting in an older wooden chair asked what he wanted.

"A beer."

"Only sell one kind. It's in that tub over there – iced down. Cold as hell. You won't find a colder or better beer on this island."

"What kind?"

"Only got one kind – Key West. It's good. Opener's there on that string."

Ira walked over, grabbed one and used the opener.

"You can set in that chair there, if you want. Take a load off."

"Thanks. You a Whidden?"

"Sure as hell. Grandpa started this place in the twenties. Now it's just me and Dora. I'm Velma. She's my sister. People livin' in these million dollar condos don't like this place. But, hell, this is old Florida. People come to see old Florida, but the people in new Florida don't like it. Son-of-a-bitch is worth millions, but we won't sell. When the last Whidden draws the last breath, well ..."

Velma was correct; the beer was ice-cold and great. Ira savored it, for as long as he dared.

"Best beer I ever had, but I got to go. There's a lady over at the hotel and the last time I saw her she had a knife in her gut."

"At the Inn!"

"Yeah, it's a long story. How much do I owe you?"

"Two bucks."

Ira handed her a five. She put it into a cloth bag and came out with three ones.

He gave her back the three and a fifty,

"The fifty's for the animals."

"Oh, are you the one? Oh, they're okay. Just scared."

But she kept the fifty.

Ira stopped and inquired about the hostess who had been the recipient of Chef Petri's twelve-inch knife in her gut,

"She's in critical condition, but expected to pull through," said the manager, "I'm not happy with what you did. Why didn't you tell us you were coming?"

"I'm not happy either. If she makes it, tell her it was my fault. I thought he'd make a run if he knew I was coming. I couldn't get any help from the local authorities – and he did run when he saw me. But I wouldn't do it again."

A thorough search of Chef Henri's cottage turned up nothing concerning the death of Mayor McCormack and his nephew, Freddie Casperson.

Ira drove slowly back to Sarasota. He purposely did not look for the place where the alligator attack happened or the spot of the altercation with the now dead cracker – who probably was someone's husband and someone's father. Sad.

It was dark when he got back to the motel. He showered, changed clothes and walked over to Michael's On East. He was starving. He ordered two filet mignons and all the trimmings. When asked about dessert he inquired about key lime pie,

"Yes, sir, we have it."

"I'll take one."

He carried it back to the hotel and ate it all before going to bed. He smoked two Roi Tans, also.

Ira booked the seven a.m. flight out of Sarasota. He was in Detroit by two. He drove the Cherokee straight to the Mackinac Straits Hospital in St. Ignace. He arrived just as Juliet was having dinner. She smiled broadly when he walked in,

"Oh, Ira, I'm so glad you're back. I was really worried. I guess from last time. I didn't know if I'd ever see you again," then the smile turned to tears of joy.

"You're not gonna' believe what happened."

CHAPTER NINETEEN

Though the Town Crier was supposed to be published just once in October, Leasil Leggett ran an extra. The headlines read:

GRAND'S CHEF HENRI PETRI KILLED
IN FREAK ACCIDENT
VICTIM OF SHARK ATTACK IN FLORIDA

Chef Henri Petri was killed in a bizarre accident in southern Florida. Petri was the head chef at the Grand Hotel. Police Chief, Ira Dempsey, had gone to Boca Grande, Florida, to question Petri regarding the murders of Mayor Kathyrn McCormack and her Nephew, Fred "Freddie" Casperson. Petri fled the
....

The paper carried the color photo that Kippi Schwartz had taken. Leasil Leggett paid the Englewood Sun one-thousand dollars for the right to do so,

"Damned expensive," Leasil was quoted as saying, "but I thought the Crier's readers deserved to see it."

The following week Juliet was released from the hospital. She rented a small two bedroom apartment – ground floor – in St. Ignace. She and Deucey Too moved in. She hired a housekeeper and arranged for a therapist to come in daily and work her arm and leg. To keep busy and her mind off her pain Juliet, as Della Queen, started an exciting novel combining her experiences both in the Mackinac to Chicago race and what had occurred in Boca Grande. It was entitled "Fools Rush In". Three months to the day from the amputation Juliet was fitted with a prosthesis. The new kind are not pretty but they are very functional. She stayed on at the apartment while she learned to walk with it. Ira visited her every day possible.

In November, Kirby Kitchen ran for mayor for the eighteenth time. He was unopposed. Only one-hundred thirteen people voted. For everyone except Kirby the job had a stigma attached to it,

"There's a lot to be done on this island and I'm going to get at it."

Just prior to Christmas, Juliet completed her novel. Her agent said it was the best work she'd ever done. Her publisher agreed and was sorry they couldn't get it printed in time for Christmas,

"We'll shoot for Valentines Day."

Arnold's keeps the ferry service going all year. On the day before Christmas Ira drove the squad car onto the first ferry leaving the island. He picked up Juliet and Deucey Too and brought them home. On the twenty-second and twenty-third Janet Phinney, Darlene Wilder and a couple of other women decorated Juliet's house for Christmas. They put candles in every window and a large wreath on the door. Upstairs in front of the four by six window that overlooked Jacker Point they decorated a small Christmas tree. In the den was a fifteen foot blue spruce, magnificent. Ira had to pay a fortune for it as it had been growing in a local's back yard for twenty years. The guy did not want to part with it and Ira had to give him enough to pay for a good-sized replacement. The ladies had decorated it very simply – large red velvet bows, an extra-large one at the top. They gathered a bunch of large pine cones, sprayed them with white flock and hung them with red pipe cleaners. They had started a fire as soon as Ira had boarded the ferry – all apple wood and it was sputtering, snapping and simmering. It was a clear day, cold and a foot of old snow on the ground. But they were going to have a white Christmas.

Ira drove as near the front door as possible,

"I want to walk the steps myself." She did but when Ira opened the door and before Juliet had taken more than a few steps Acey came bounding in from the den yelping and barking and making noises that Juliet had never heard before. He jumped up, hit Juliet with his two front paws and sent her sprawling. Acey was all over her, barking, yelping and licking her. Juliet was bawling and Acey was licking her tears,

"Oh, Acey, Acey! You old thing. I missed you so." And Ira let her sit there and cry. After a few minutes he offered her his hand,

"I want to get up myself." She did and Darlene, Janet and the rest of the girls hugged her and made a great fuss over her.

Ira got Deucey Too out of the squad car, brought her into the house and introduced her to Acey. Acey just sniffed her from one end to the other, accepted her and then crowded over to Juliet who was trying to get to the den. The ladies stayed all day and made lunch and a general fuss. They left the two of them alone in the late afternoon.

"Can we go to church tonight? It's Christmas Eve," asked Juliet.

"Of course we can."

They attended midnight services at the Little Stone Congregational Church. It's not a large church but when they entered everyone stood up. There was no applause or anything like it but it was a genuine show of support and respect.

Pastor Ron Williams acknowledged their presence,

"We are happy to have Chief Dempsey and Miss Juliet Steinbrenner worship with us on this most joyful night as we prepare to celebrate the birth of our king and savior, Jesus Christ."

The congregation in unison gave an "Amen".

They drove back to Juliet's in the squad car. They sat in front of the fireplace and enjoyed a glass of wine – one dog snuggled on either side of Juliet. Ira sat in one of the great leather chairs.

Very early Christmas morning she took his hand,

"Will you help me up the staircase?"

"Of course." He carried her.

She took off her clothes and prosthesis. Naked, she crawled into bed, "Oh, how I've missed this bed."

"Me, too."

They lay there a while holding hands, then he caressed her whole body, every inch including the scars where once her beautiful leg had been. As they lie there Ira could still picture the day she first walked into his office, furious over the pranks of the Freeman twins, dressed in riding attire and taping her left boot with her riding crop. Never to be done again,

"Will this hurt the baby?"

"I don't think she'll mind and I know I won't."

"How do you know it's a girl?"

"Ira, how long was I in the hospital?"

They made love as if for the first time.

CHAPTER TWENTY

Ira and Juliet were married during the Lilac Festival. They were married outdoors in Marquette Park which had been upgraded considerably by Mayor Kirby Kitchen. The weather gods smiled on the event. Tourists were invited by announcements in the Town Crier, by proclamation of the Mayor and by flyers plastered all over town. Many attended though they had no idea who was getting married or of the circumstances surrounding the occasion. Nearly every islander attended.

Juliet wore the traditional white gown. It was not only beautiful but billowy enough to hide her seven month pregnancy. She looked radiant. Ira wore a tuxedo and cut a good figure in it,

"I'm only going to get married once."

Clyde Stone was Ira's best man. Dickerson and Upland served as groomsmen. Rosetta Stone was the matron of honor and Darlene and Janet were bridesmaids. The dining room hostess at the Gasparilla Inn survived the knife wound. Ira and Juliet flew her and her husband to Mackinac first class and set them up in a suite at the Grand. Doctor Richard Florian flew up from Englewood and stood beaming as he watched the ceremonies from the first row. Juliet threw her bouquet to the crowd of single ladies and it was caught by Caitlin Smart, Miss Lilac of the year before and hostess at the Island House. Rosetta Stone caught Ira's eye and smiled. Ira just shrugged his shoulders. Juliet elected to put her garter on the leg with the prosthesis. When Ira knelt to take it off and raised her skirt people whistled at her artificial leg. After the wedding everyone was invited to the reception held up at old Fort Mackinac. Nearly everyone attended.

The headlines of the Town Crier read:
SOCIALITE WEDS CHIEF
ISLANDS BIGGEST EVENT IN YEARS

Islander native and socialite, Juliet Steinbrenner, was married this past Sunday to the island's police chief, Ira Dempsey. The new Mrs. Dempsey is the granddaughter of Charles Steinbrenner who spent many years on the island crafting fine sailing boats. Chief Dempsey came to our island .....

Afterward Ira thought of retirement. He'd had enough excitement to last a lifetime. He thought it would be nice to stay home and help Juliet raise a family.

Juliet had other ideas, "I love you to death, but I'm almost thirty-nine. I don't think I want any more children. This one will be a blessing. If you retire what are you going to do – ride horses, sail boats and smoke cigars? That will get old in a hurry."

Ira agreed and guessed that the rest of his career would not be as exciting. It wasn't.

Slim Dickerson stayed on until his youngest child graduated from Hillsdale College.

Doug Upland resigned after Labor Day, "I've had enough of these little shits, besides I can't raise four kids on my salary."

Ira agreed the salary was low, but he did not see any money for raises coming soon. He was not sorry to see Upland go. However, he did not say so. Ira hired Ed Dickerson's oldest son, Ed Junior, who had recently graduated in criminal justice from Grand Valley.

Clyde Stone retired as mayor of Kankakee. He and Rosetta bought a small place on West Bluff. After living there two years and seeing the mess Kirby Kitchen was making as mayor he decided to run. He was elected,

"Beats the hell out of Kankakee."

In defeat Kirby stated, "I didn't want this job anyway. I only ran as I knew it would piss off Katy."

The Kathyrn McCormack/Fred Casperson file sits in Ira's bottom right hand drawer. The case remains open and active. The first thing

Ira does each day is pull out the file, pour a cup of black coffee, light up a Roi Tan and try and find the answers. Very few seasonals come to the island to work a second season. Most learn in one year. There are few to interview. Many of them have never heard of Chef Henri Petri.

Those at The Grand say nothing. Samuel Lee Eddington refused to even give Leasil Leggett an interview. Chef Who? No one has ever incriminated him. They are tight lipped people. The Grand promoted Grace McKinney to head chef. She became the first woman so named.

No one has ever been charged, no killer or killers found. The fact that Henri Petri fled at the sight of Ira has convinced many he was guilty and that justice was served by a great white shark. But, if guilty, what was his motive for killing the pair? A drug deal gone sour? Ira felt certain Freddie was bringing drugs onto the island in his backpack. If so, did he have the wits to deal them? Did he even have the wits to know he was bringing them in? Probably. He did have the wits to scrawl "CI" in his own blood.

Katy McCormack. How was she involved? Did she take the drugs from Freddie and deal them off to Chef Henri? Did Henri in turn supply the island? These questions have yet to be answered. Ira asks them each day. No one talks. No one ever implicated the mayor. Juliet has never said a word – they were dear, dear friends. *I may never know for certain.* One thing did become certain, however – after the deaths of the trio, drug use went into a complete nosedive. Marijuana and alcohol use continued as usual, but there were very few incidents where hard drugs were involved and there were no more deaths from overdose. Ira could deal with marijuana and beer, but he could not deal with another Teddy Freeman.

On June thirteenth Sassy Dempsey made her way into this world. She was a healthy seven pounds-five ounces and nineteen inches long. She had a mop of bright red hair. On the same date Doctor Richard Florian set sail alone from Englewood, Florida. He sailed south around Florida, up the eastern coast of the United States and down the Saint Lawrence Seaway. He arrived at Haldimand Bay and docked. He walked up to the visitor's center.

"Can you tell me where Juliet and Ira Dempsey live?"

He walked up the long hill to the house on Trillium Street and rang the bell. Juliet answered.

"I'm looking for a mate for the Chicago to Mackinac race. I aim to win it."

"Well, you may just be at the right place."

ABOUT THE AUTHOR

Roy Ault, was a teacher, coach. and administrator in the public schools and universities of Ohio for many years. After leaving the field of education he started a business that is still in operation. In 1986 he became a columnist for the Sun Coast Media Group and wrote for them for over 25 years. During that period he also wrote articles that were published in the Columbus Dispatch, Philadelphia Inquirer and the Tampa Tribune. He has also been published in Reminisce magazine.

Roy has written several books, all self published, including *You're Driving Me Crazy*, a humorous account of his many experiences in teaching people to drive. He also wrote *The Definitive Book For Driving School Owners,* a book dedicated to the profession he has pursued for over forty years. *Roy's Rhetoric* is a compilation of over 200 of his columns written for the Englewood Sun. *Sudden Death* chronicles an Ohio basketball team through their outstanding season of 1952 and *The Coach* takes Max Ivers from high school football coach to the Super Bowl. This is Roy's first mystery novel.

All of these books may be purchased online at Amazon.com or you order them by using the form below.

Please fill the blank in front of the book name with the number of copies you want to order. All books are $13.95 plus $3.00 each for shipping and handling.

_____Murder On Mackinac
_____Sudden Death
_____The Coach
_____Roy's Rhetoric
_____The Definitive Book For Driving School Owners
TOTAL ENCLOSED: _____

Mail order with payment to: Roy's Rhetoric
406 N. Indiana Ave., Suite 10
Englewood, FL 34223

Made in the USA
Charleston, SC
31 January 2016